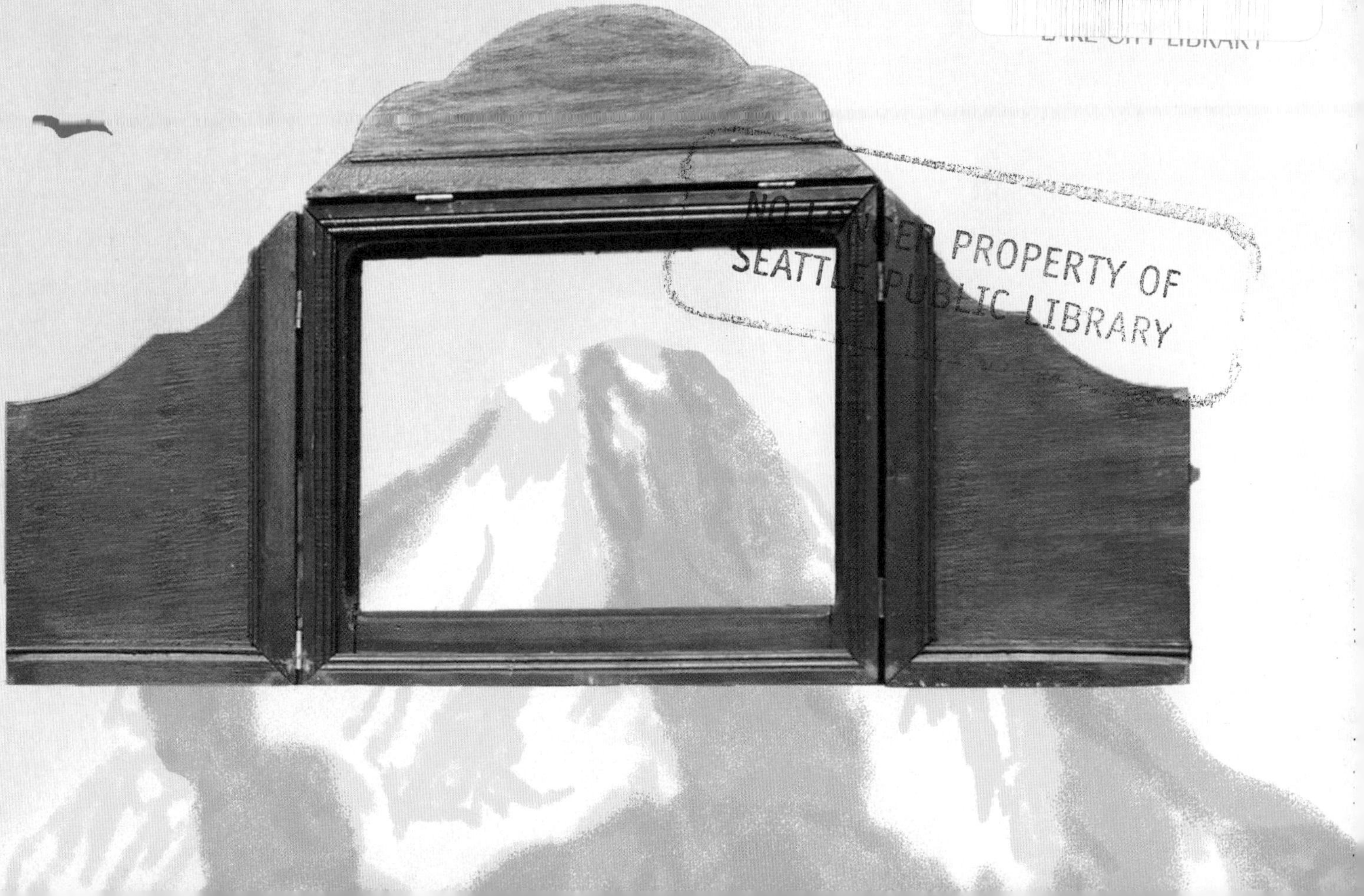

In memory of David A. Berona, friend and colleague, who taught us that pictures speak volumes.

Editorial Director: FRANÇOISE MOULY

Design: JAMES STURM & FRANÇOISE MOULY

JAMES STURM'S artwork was drawn with pen and brush in India ink and colored digitally.

 All our books are Smyth Sewn (the highest library-quality binding available) and printed with soy-based inks on acid-free, woodfree paper harvested from responsible sources. Printed in China by C&C Offset Printing Co., Ltd. Distributed to the trade by Consortium Book Sales; orders (800) 283-3572; orderentry@perseusbooks.com; www.cbsd.com.

Library of Congress Cataloging-in-Publication Data: Sturm, James, 1965- Birdsong : a story in pictures / James Sturm. pages cm Summary: "The wordless adventure of two children whose misdeeds are punished when they're transformed into monkeys. In the tradition of kamishibai, or Japanese paper theater, the wordless format gives freedom to the readers to tell the story as they see it."– Provided by publisher. ISBN 978-1-935179-94-8 (hardcover : alk. paper) 1. Graphic novels. [1. Graphic novels. 2. Conduct of life--Fiction. 3. Monkeys--Fiction. 4. Shapeshifting--Fiction. 5. Stories without words.] I. Title. PZ7.7.S84Bi 2016 741.5'973--dc23 2015029258

ISBN 13: 978-1-935179-94-8 (hardcover)

16 17 18 19 20 21 22 C&C 10 9 8 7 6 5 4 3 2 1

A TOON BOOK

www.TOON-BOOKS.com

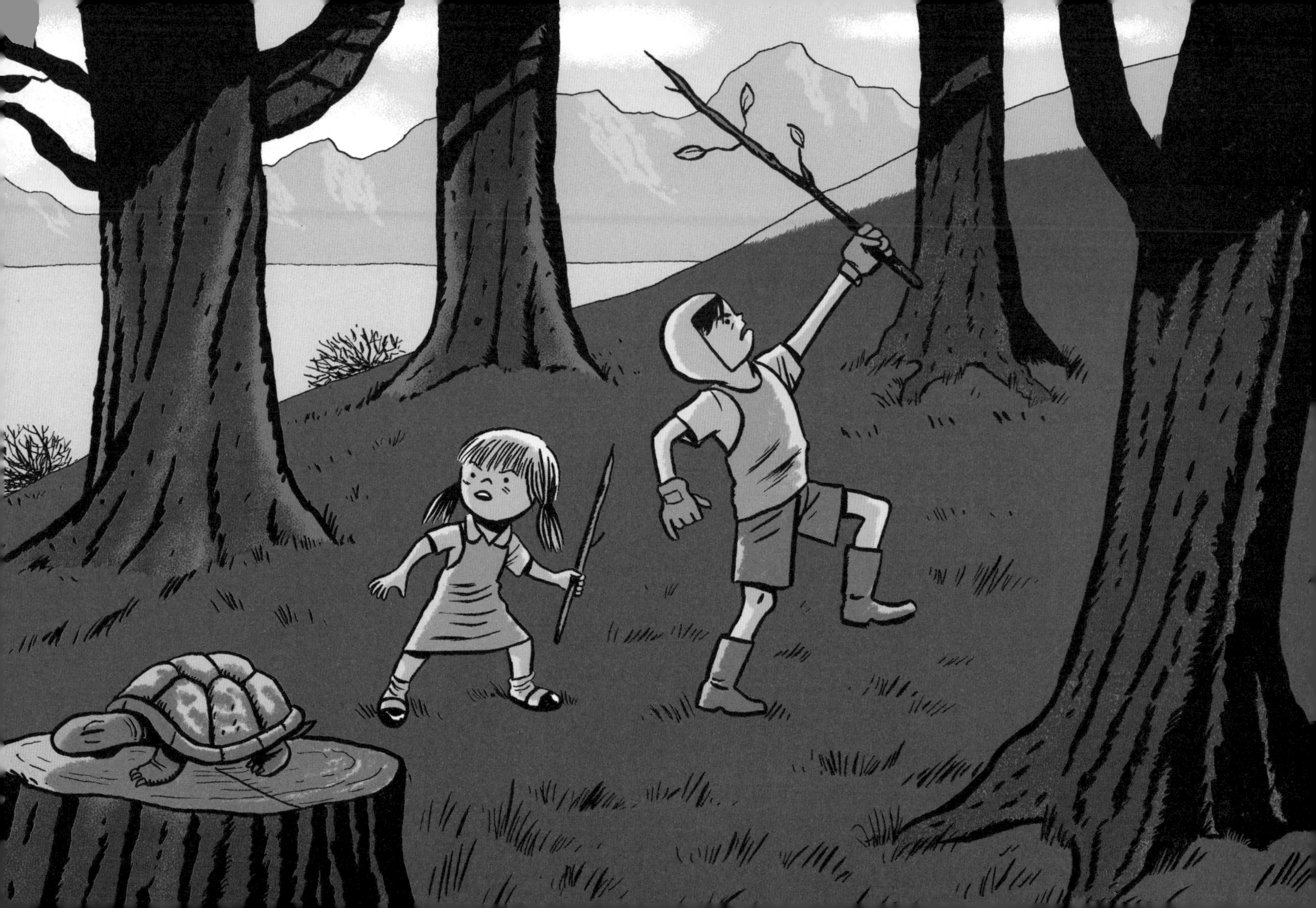

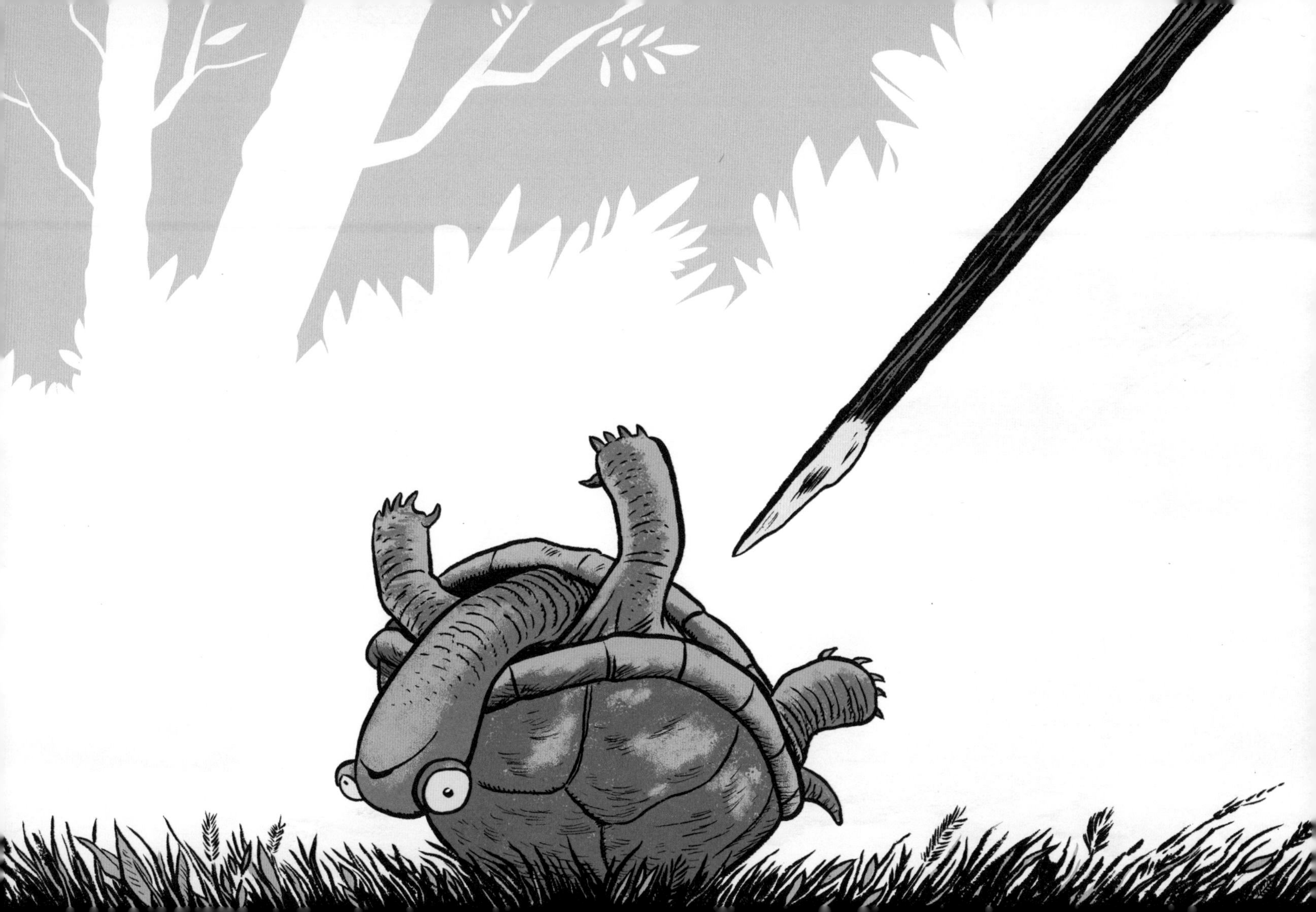

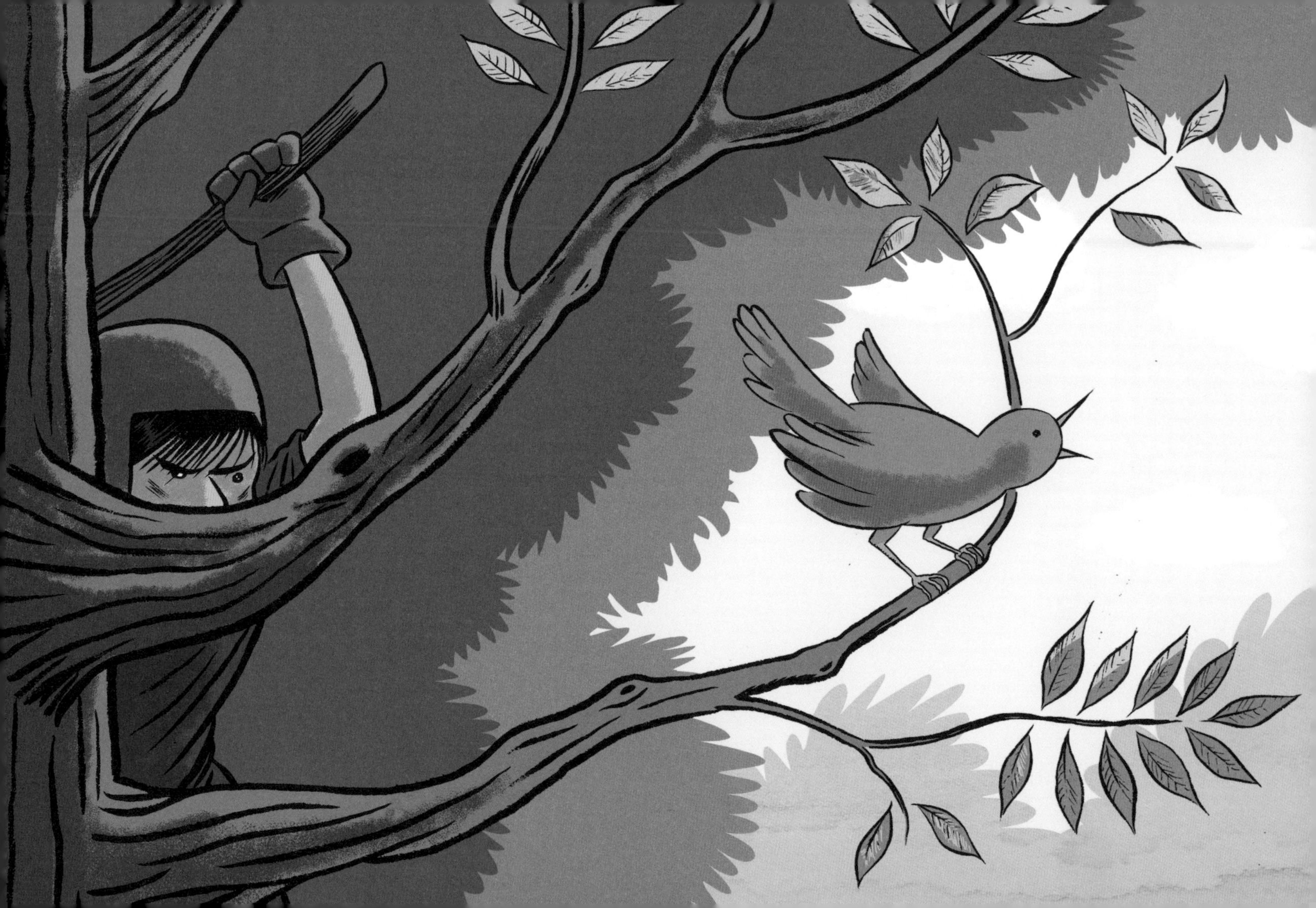

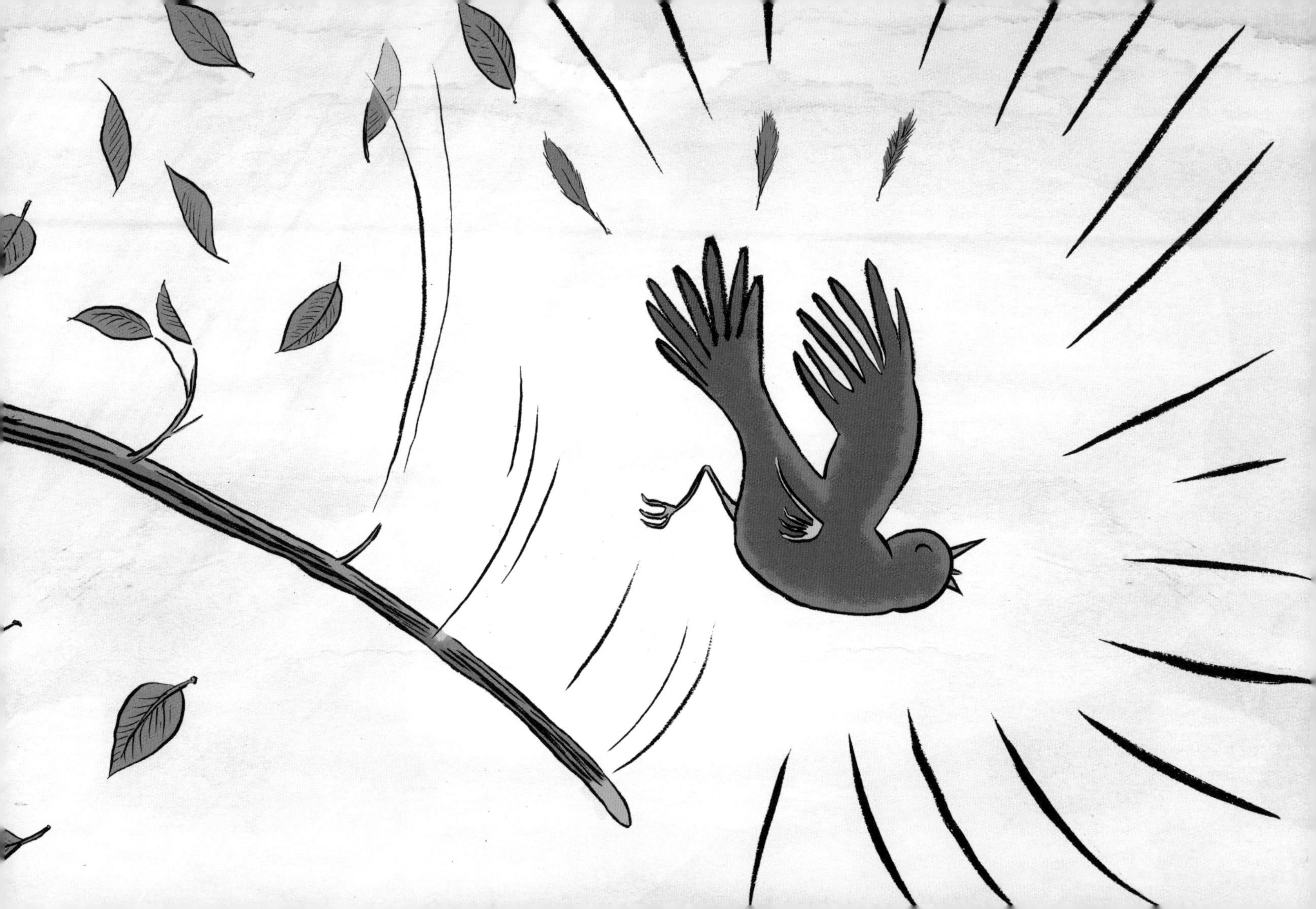

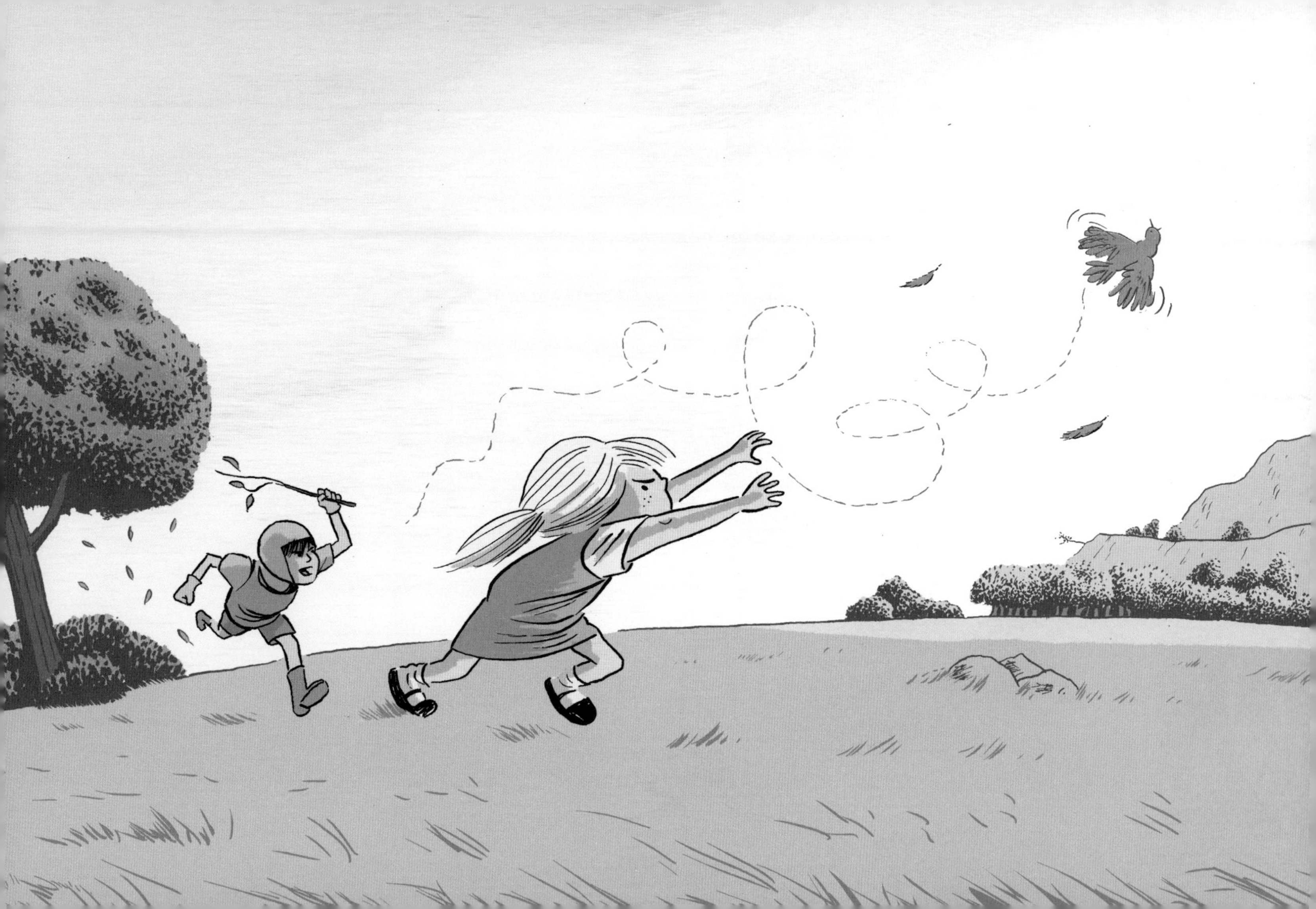

14

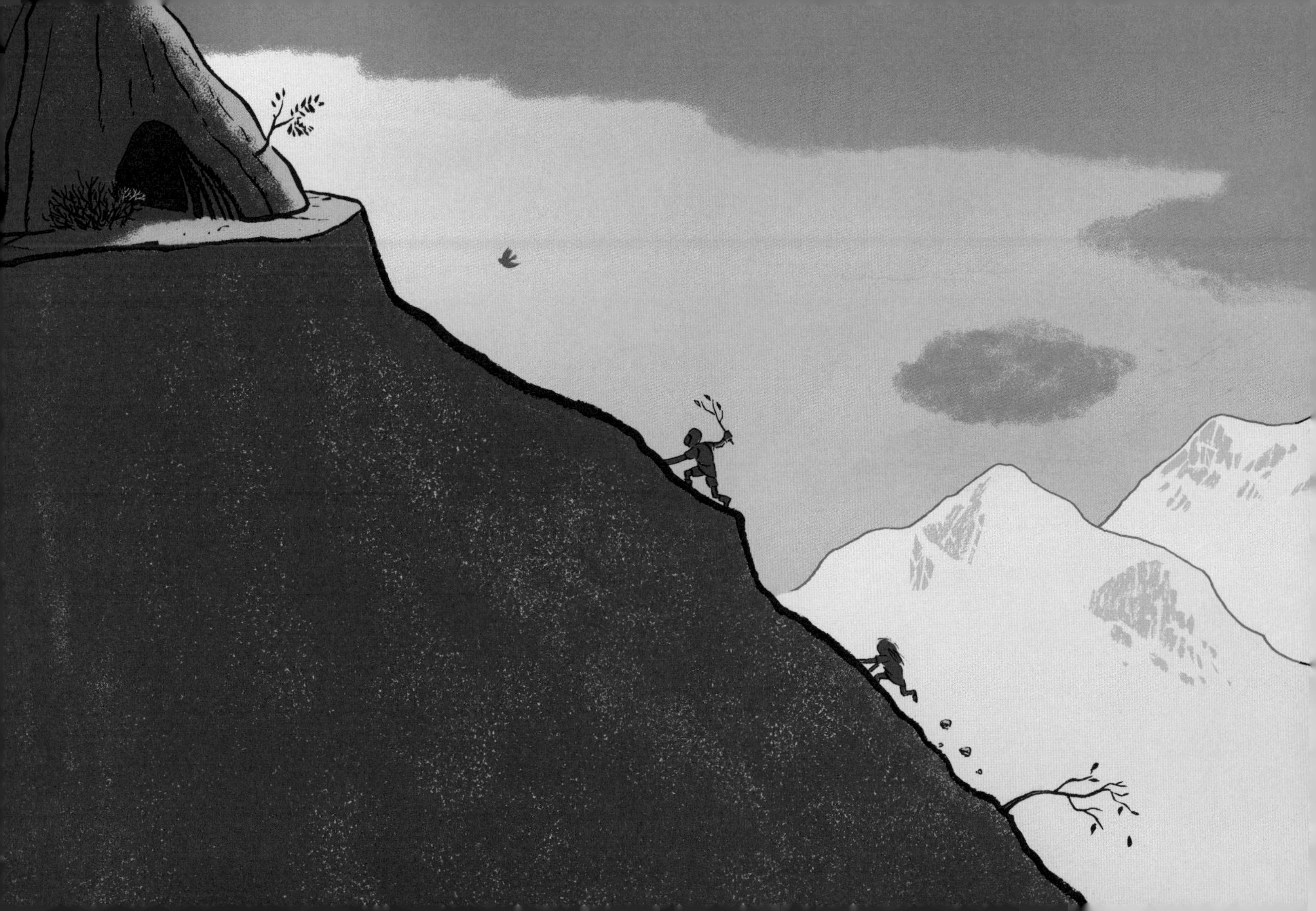

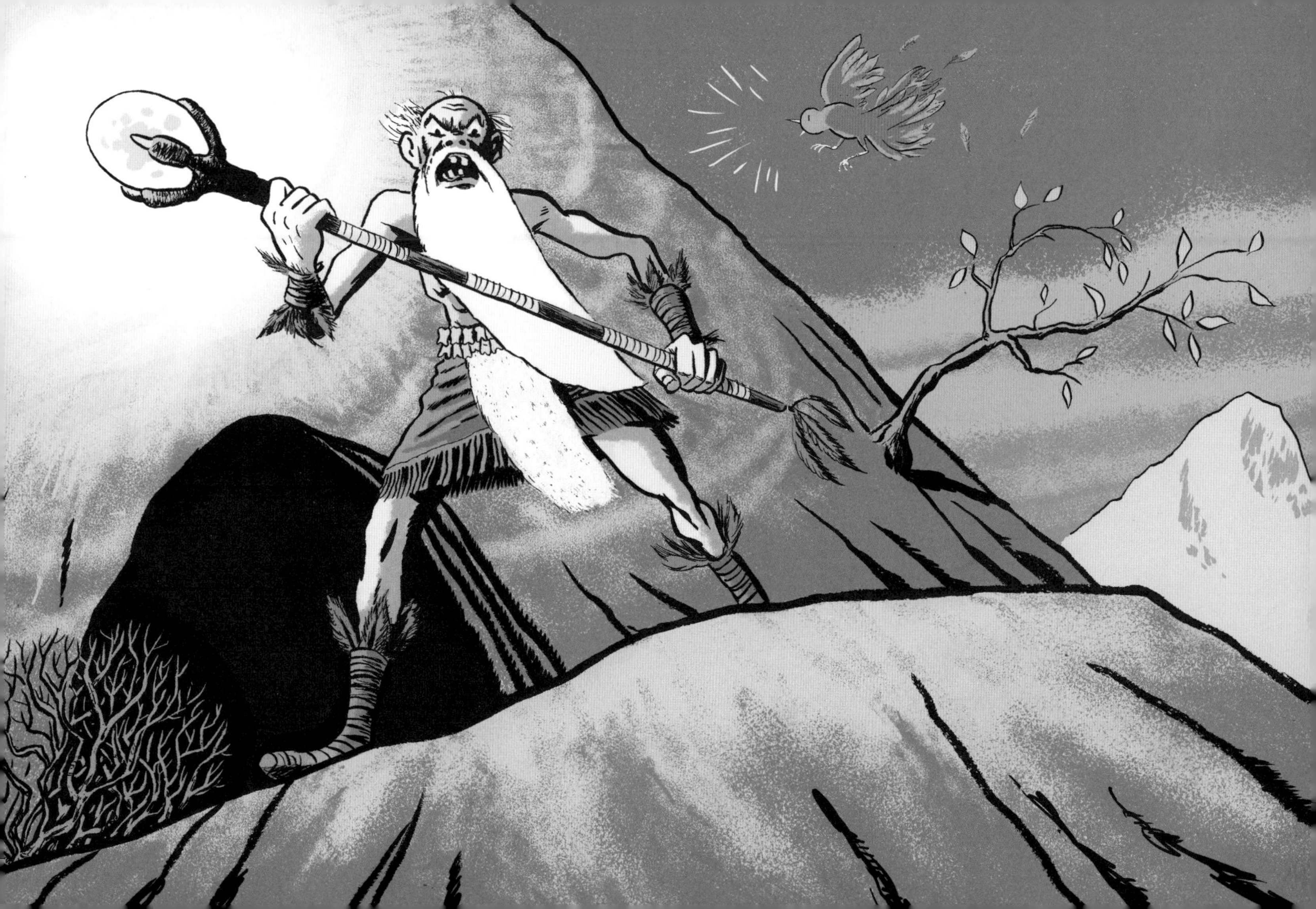

18

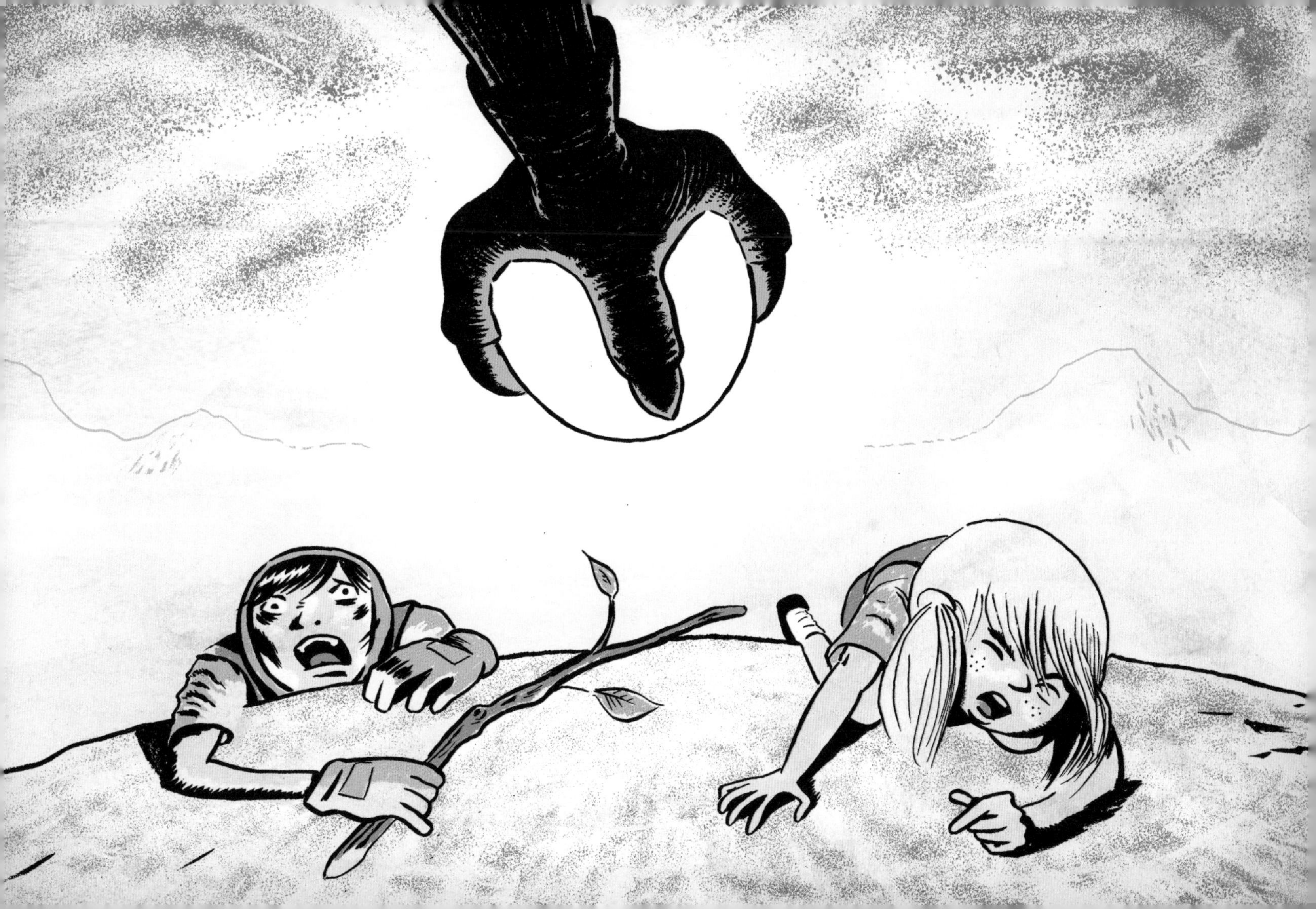

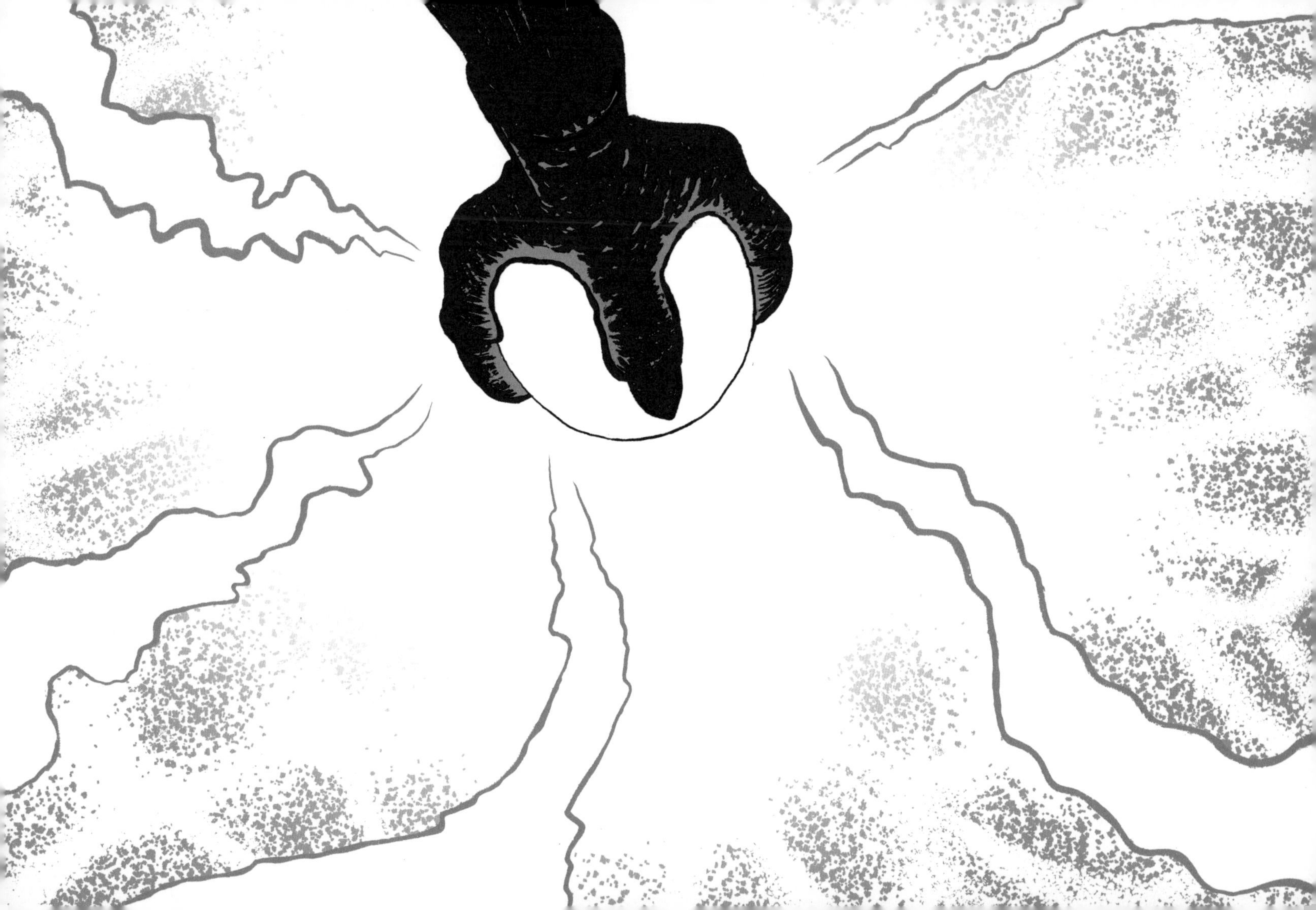

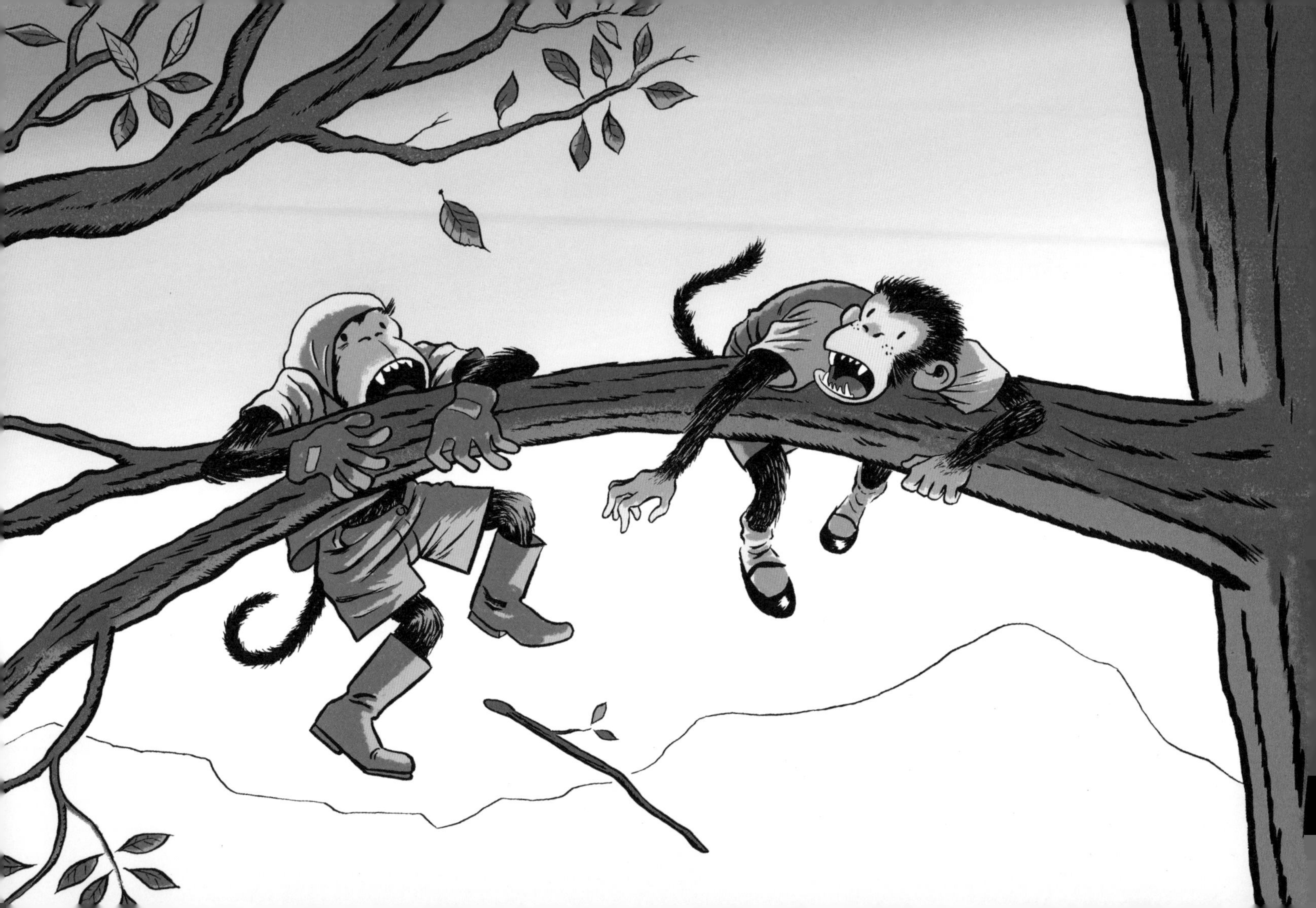

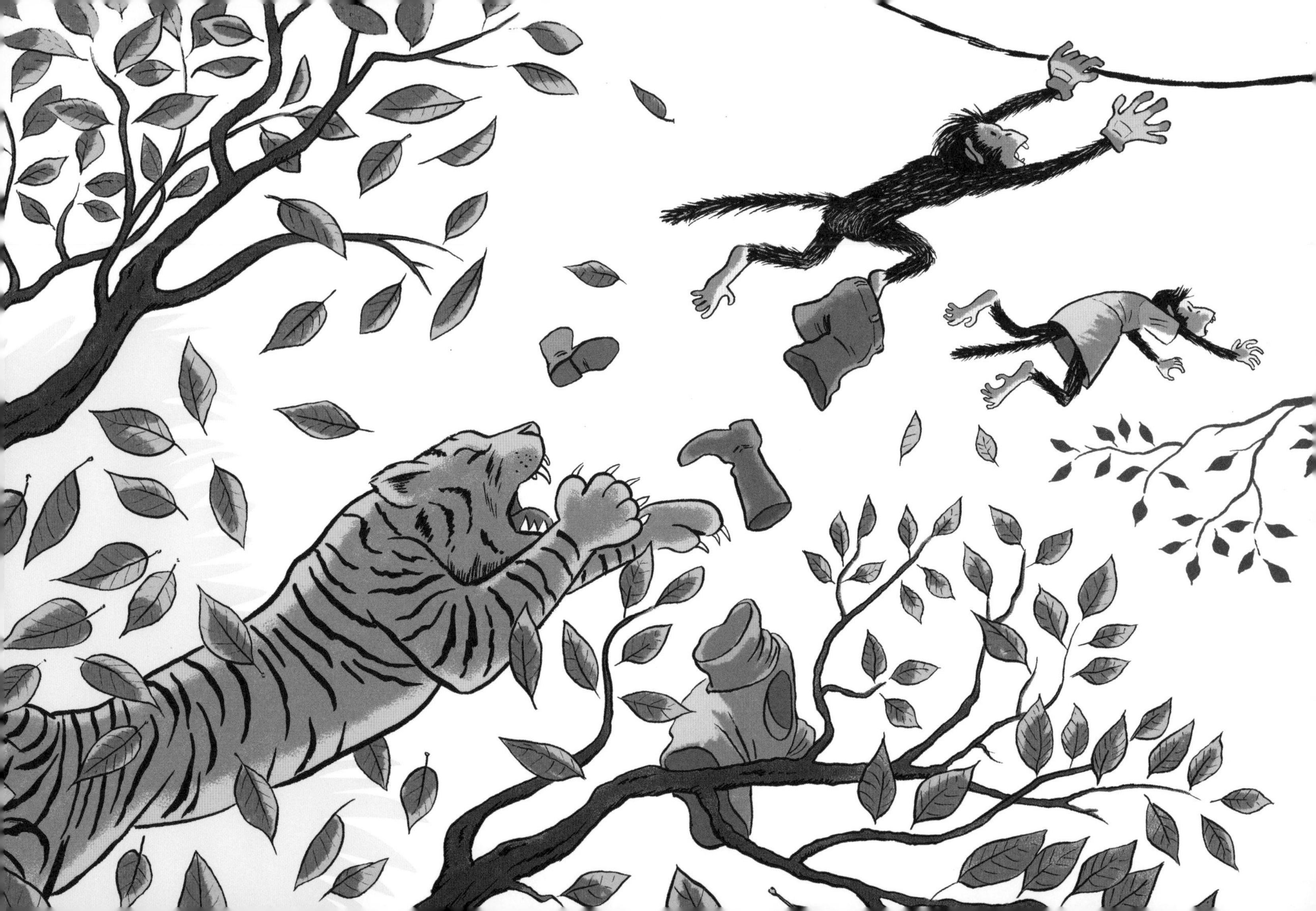

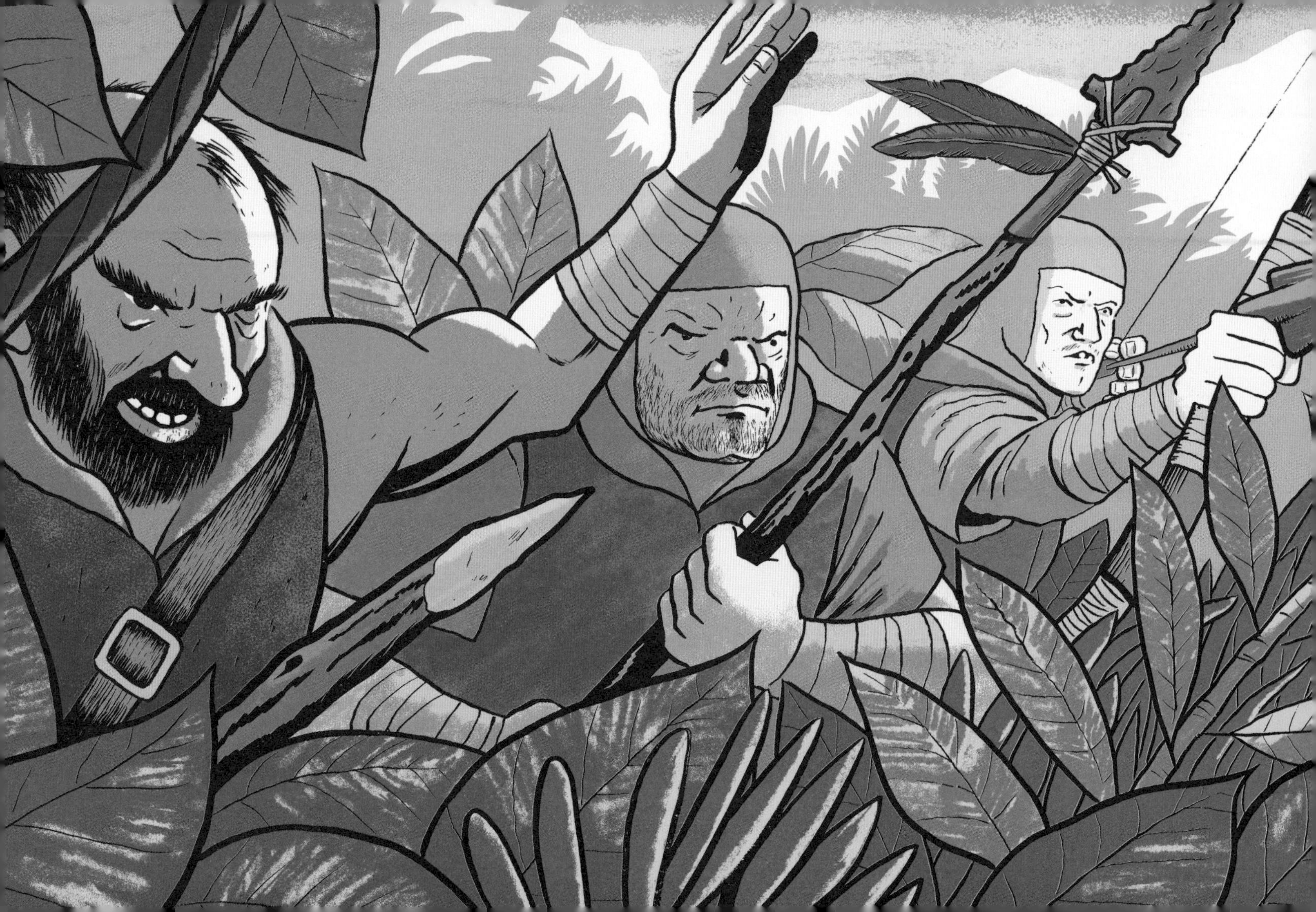

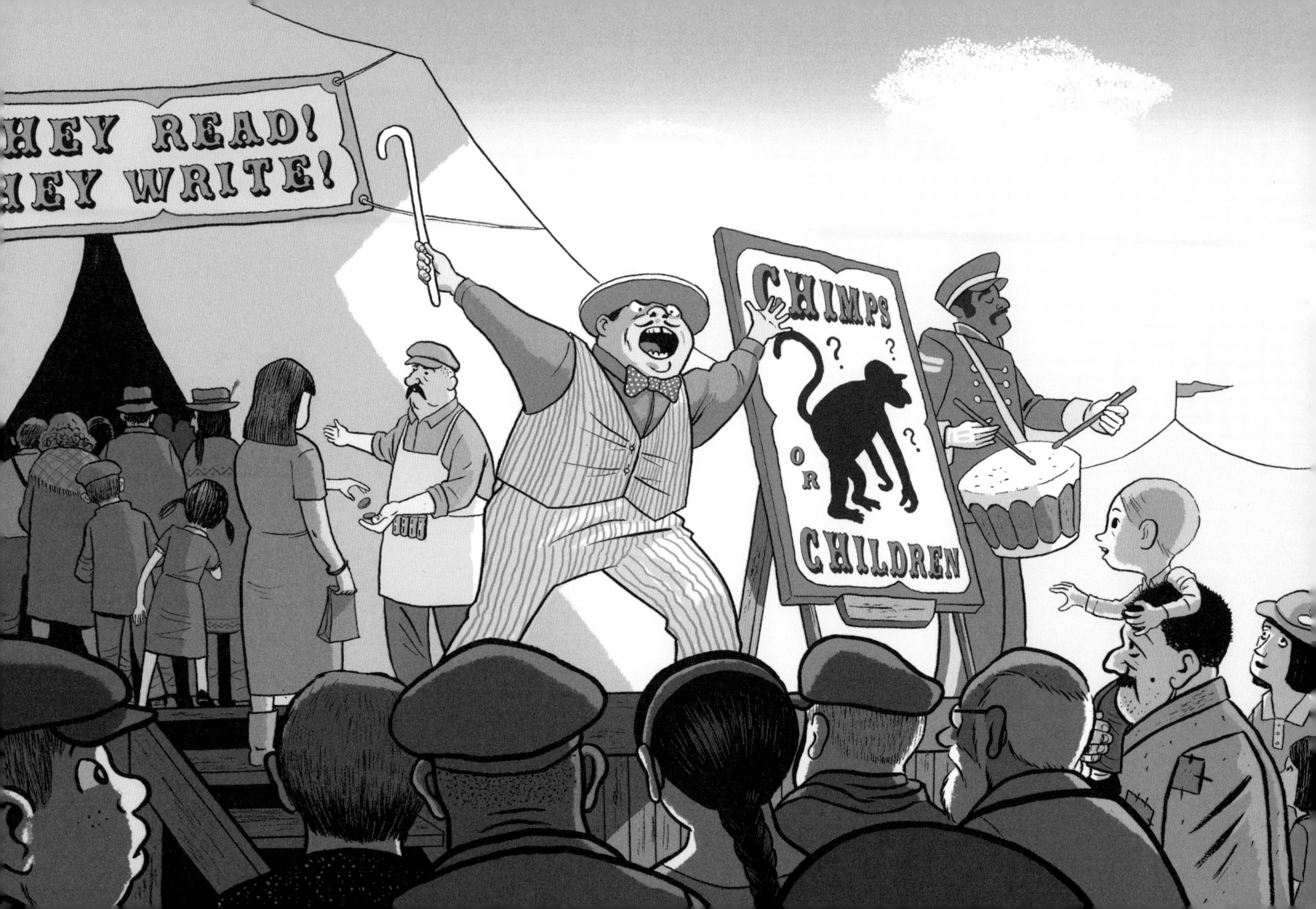
HEY READ!
HEY WRITE!
CHIMPS
OR
CHILDREN

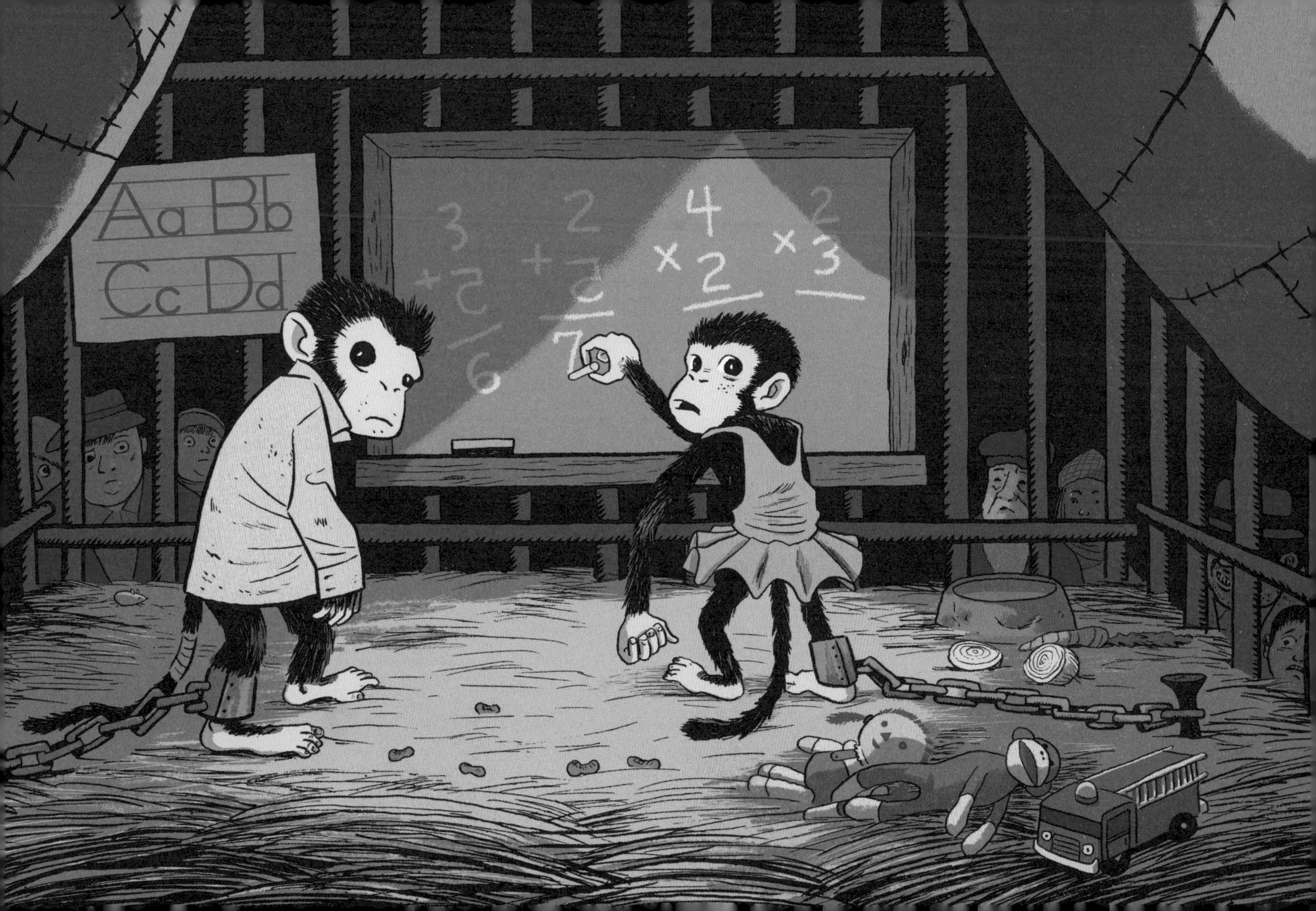
Aa Bb
Cc Dd
3 +2 6
2 +2 7
4 ×2
2 ×3

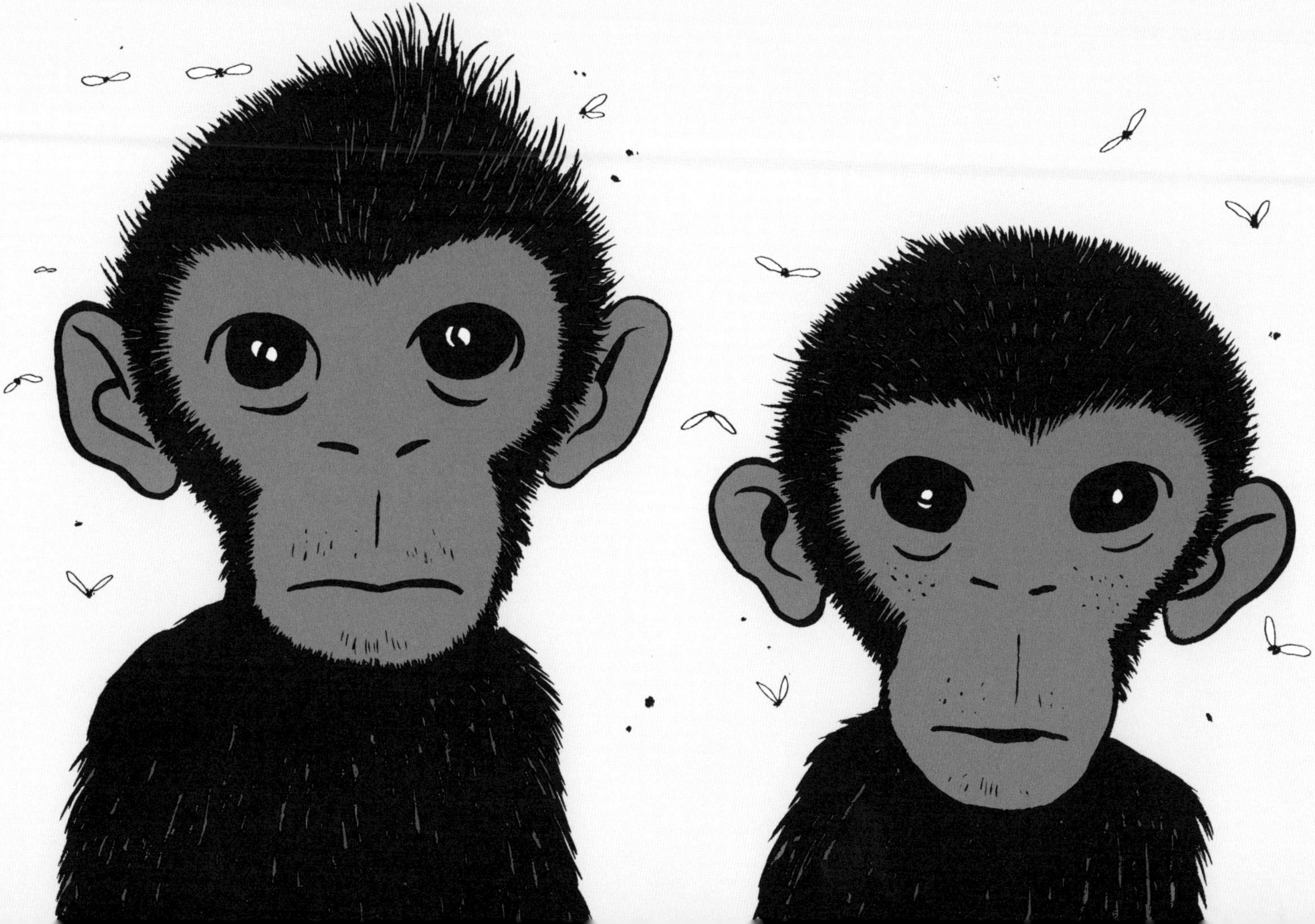

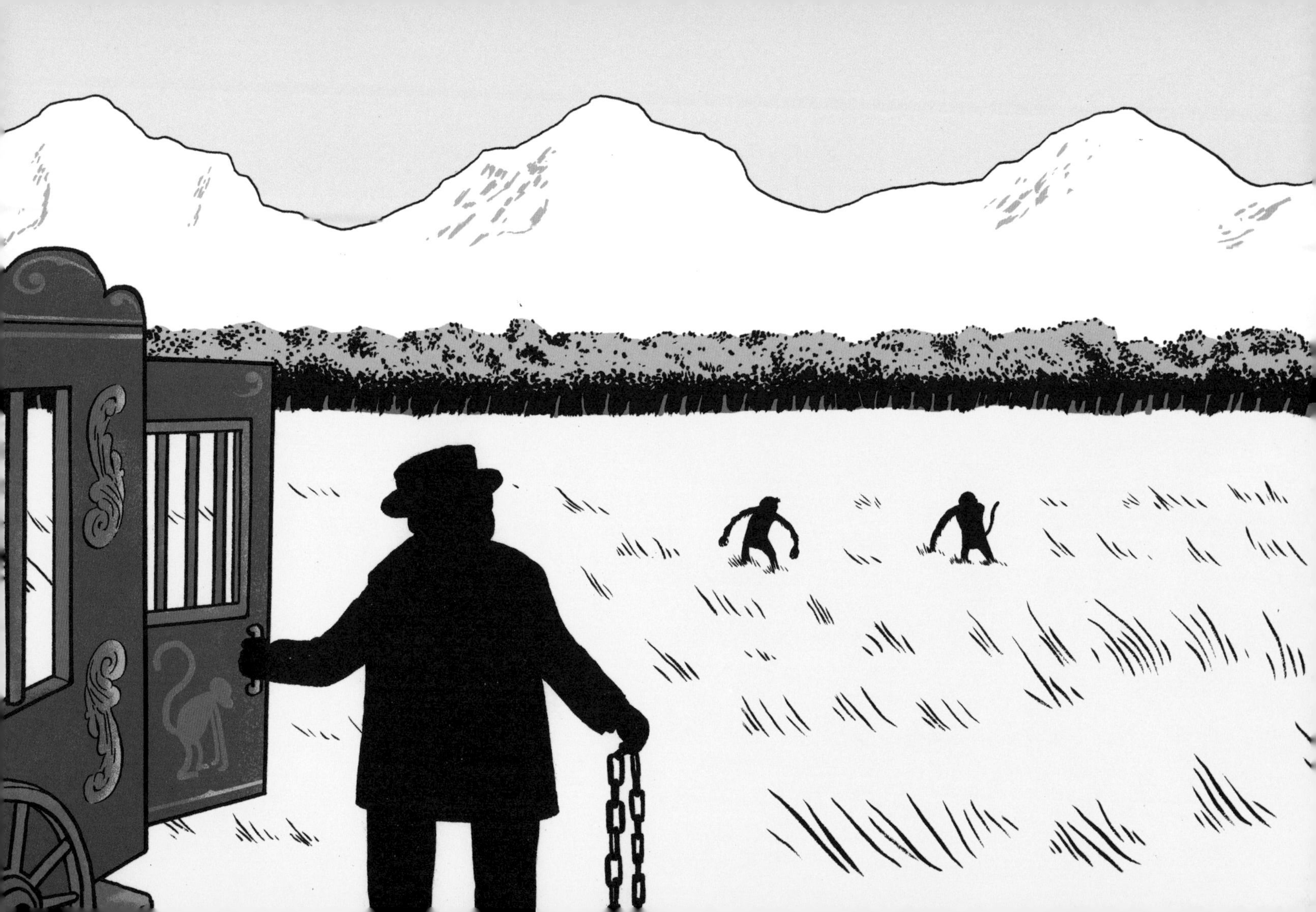

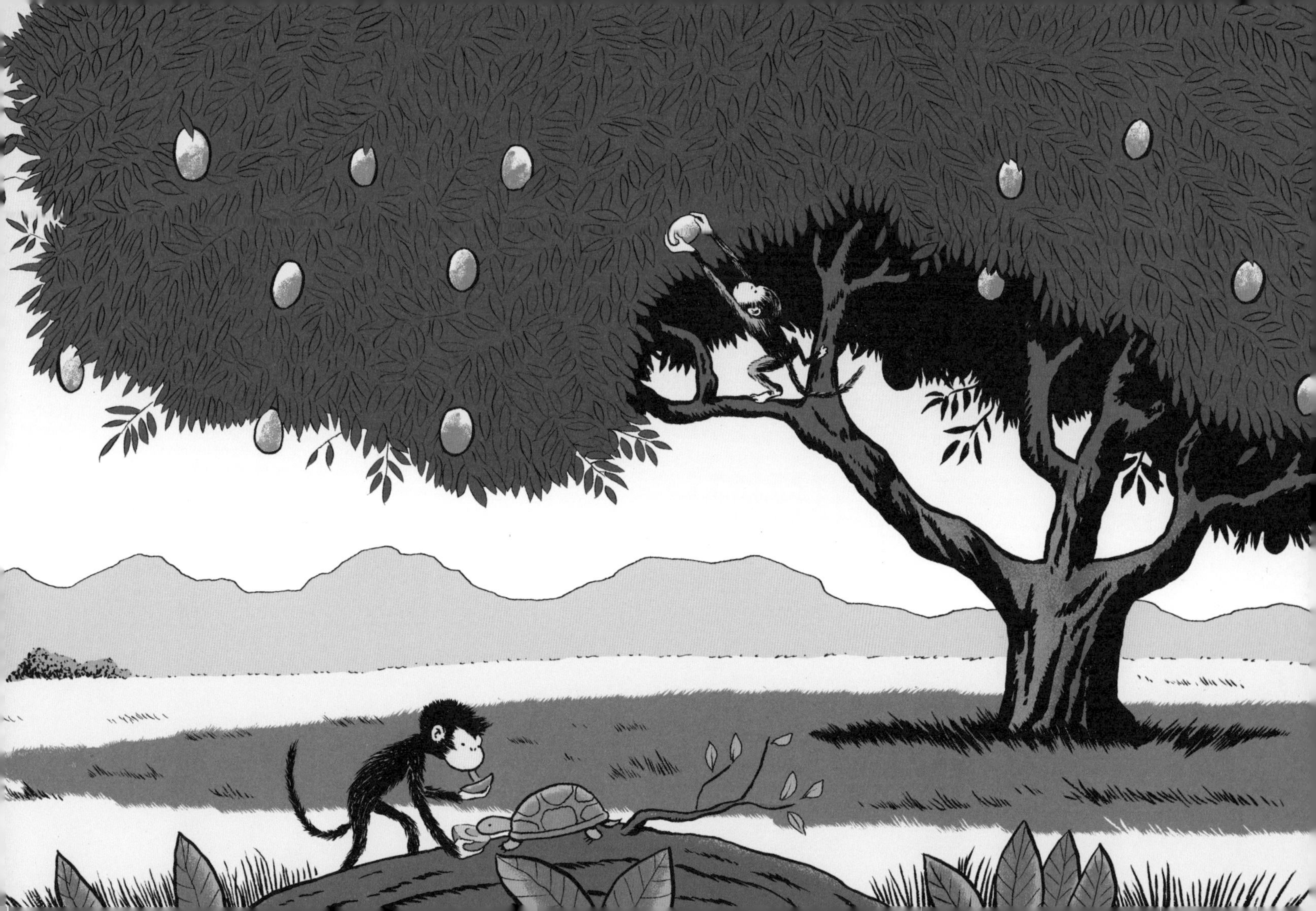

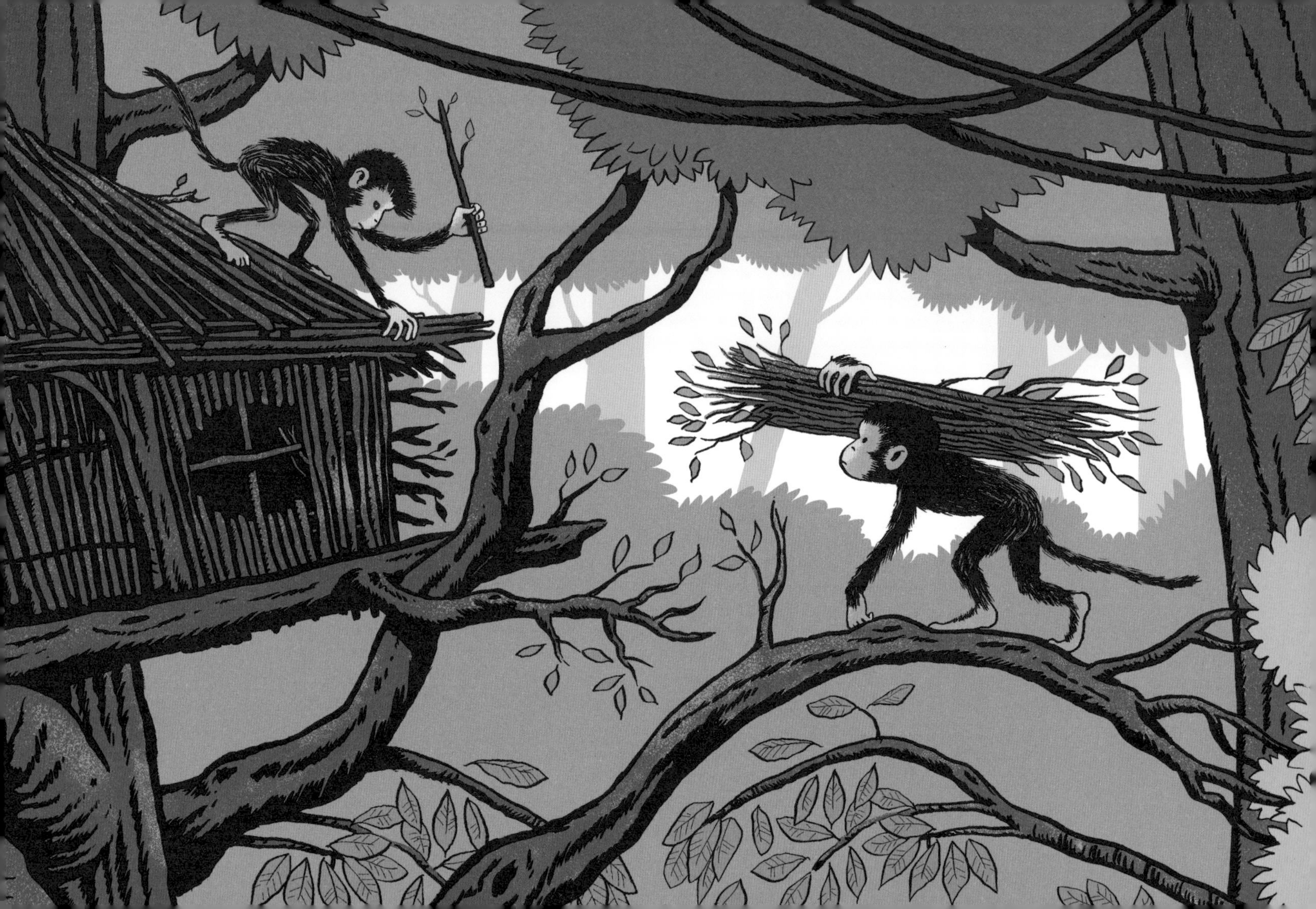

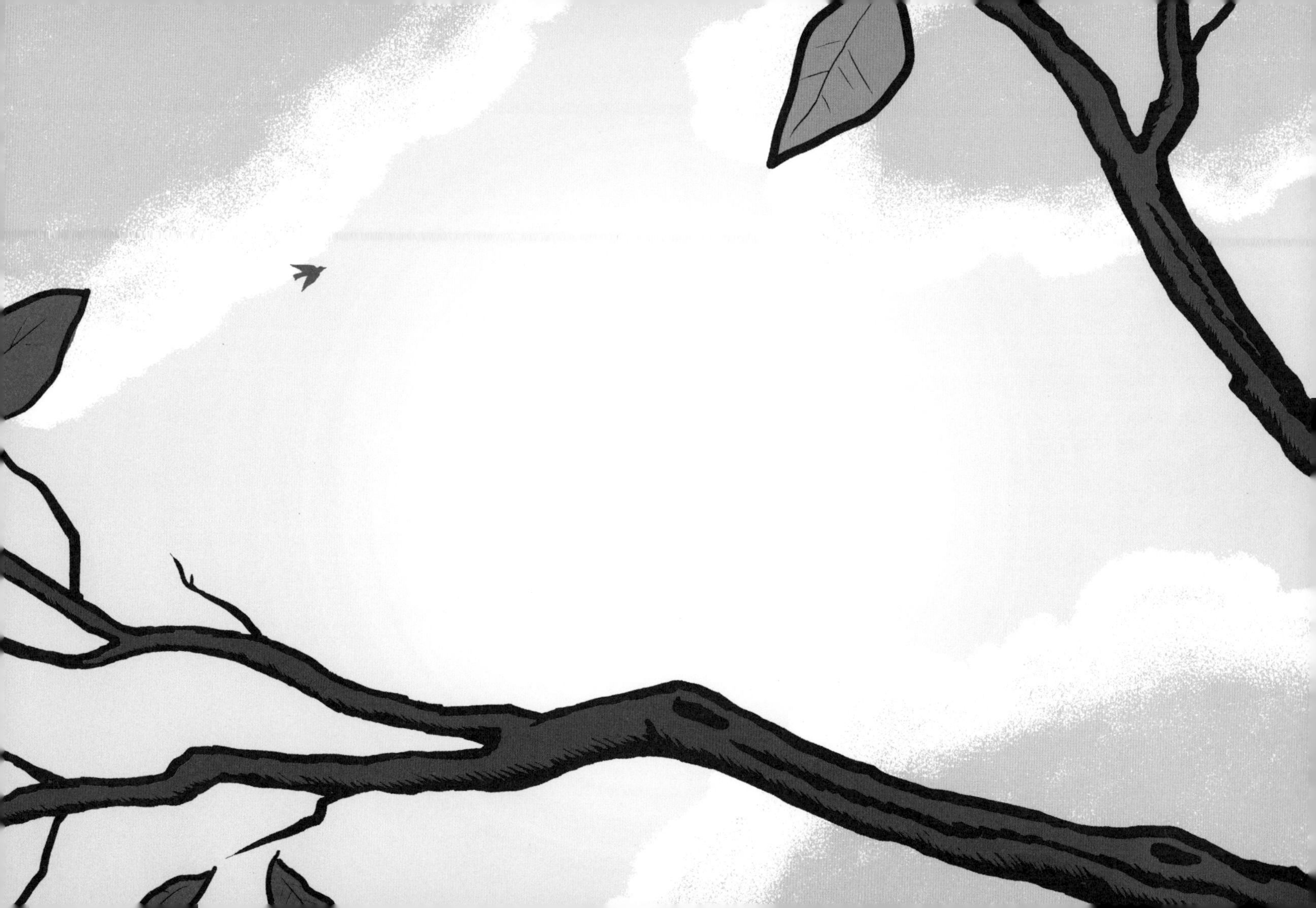

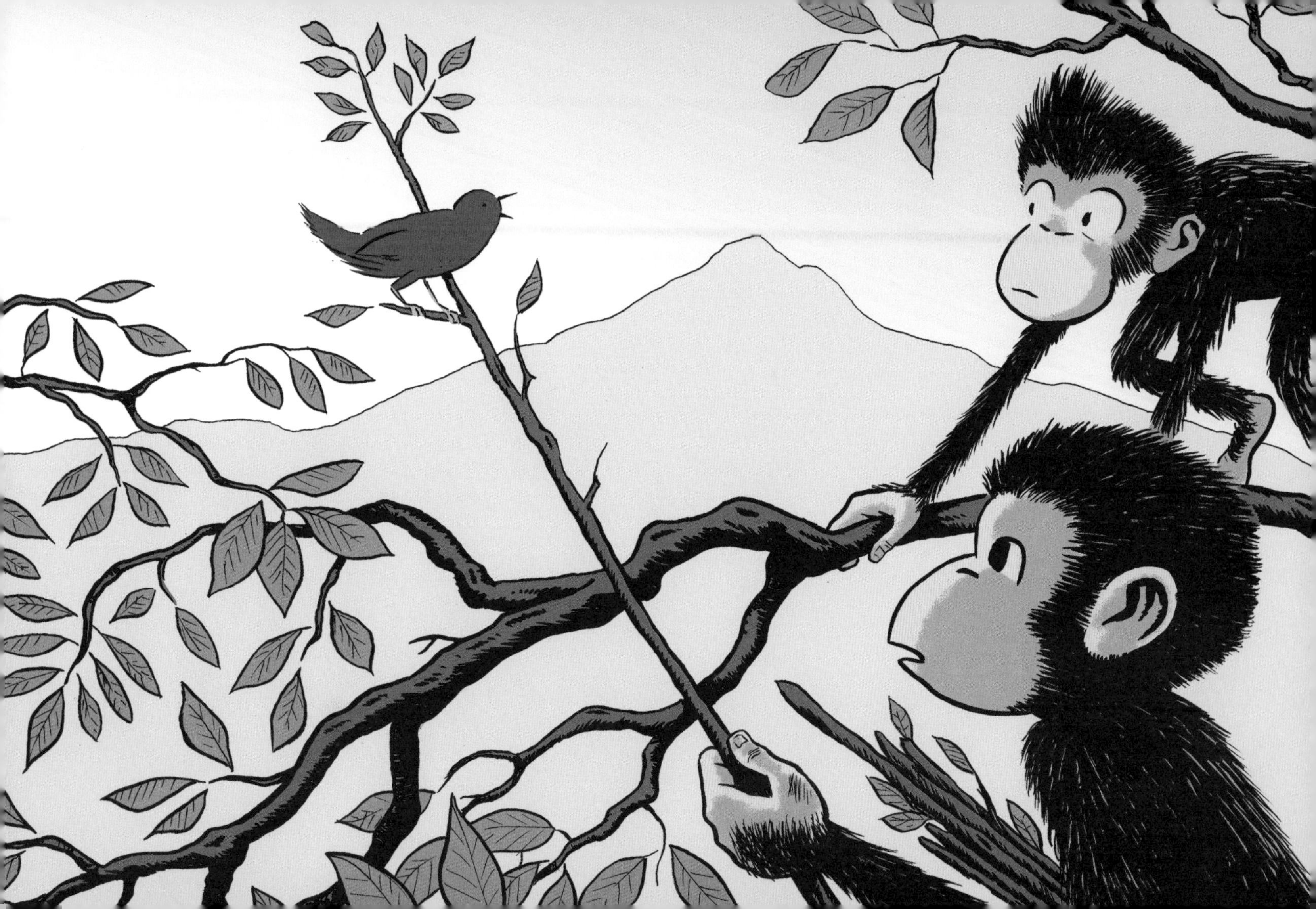

44

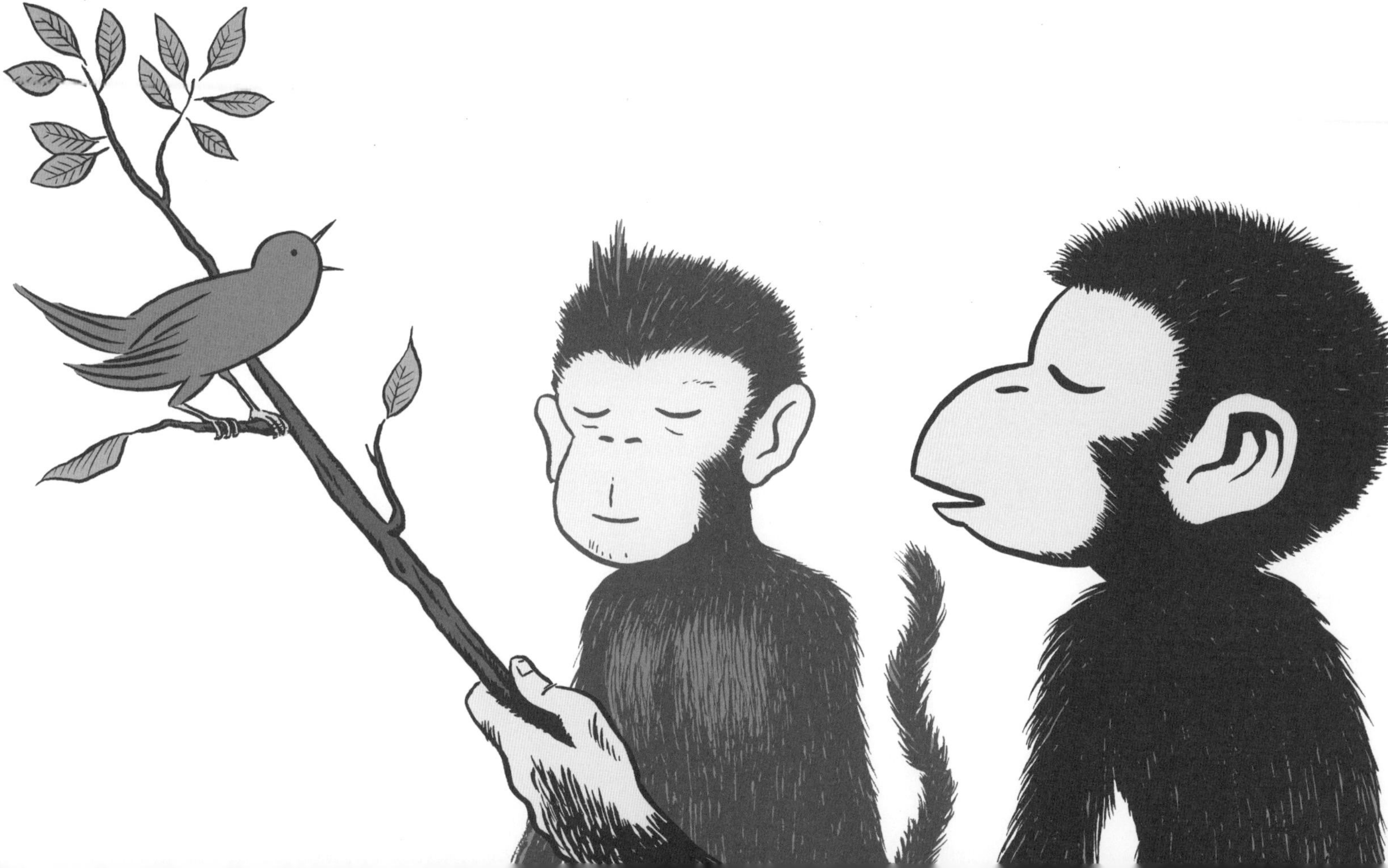

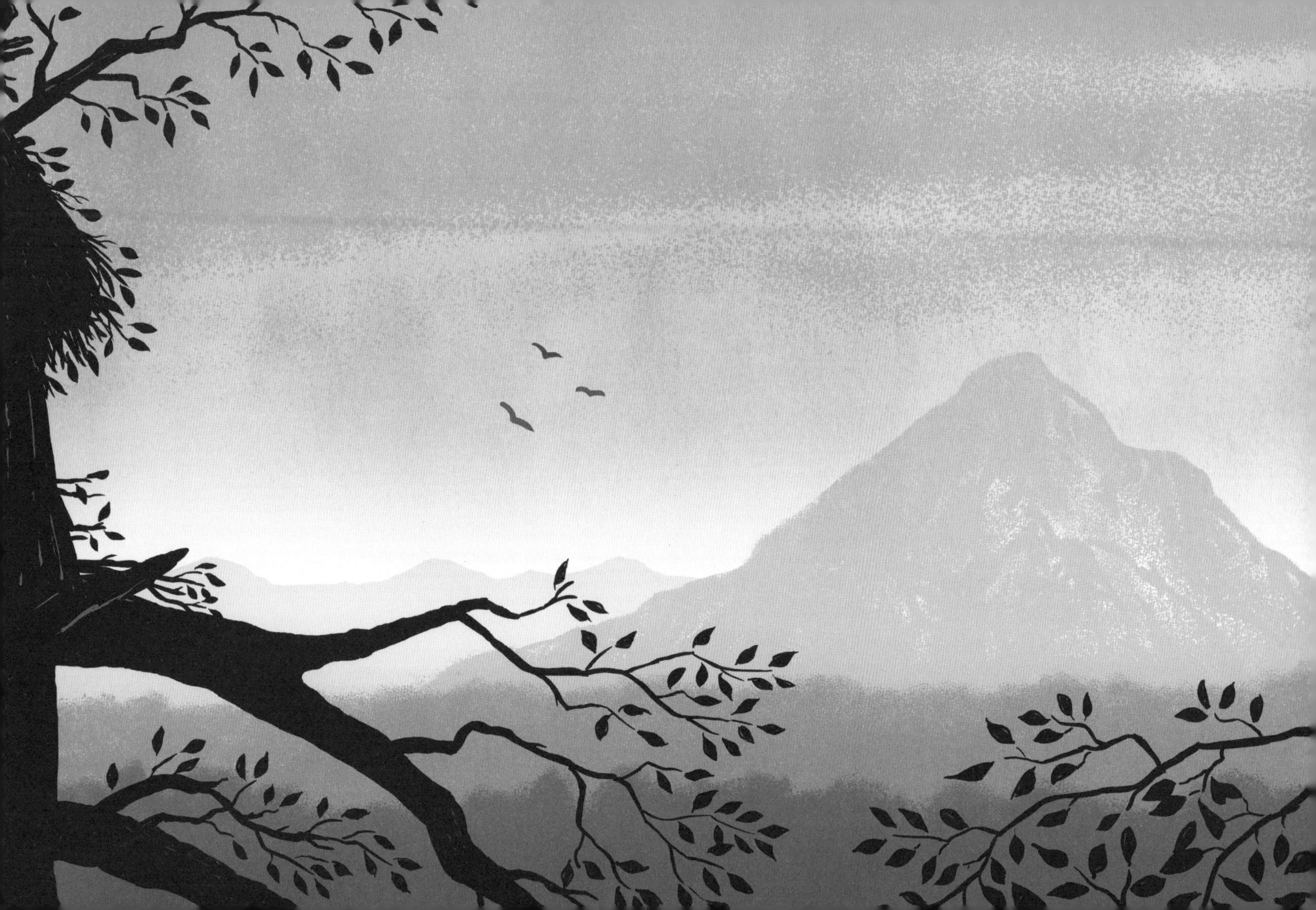

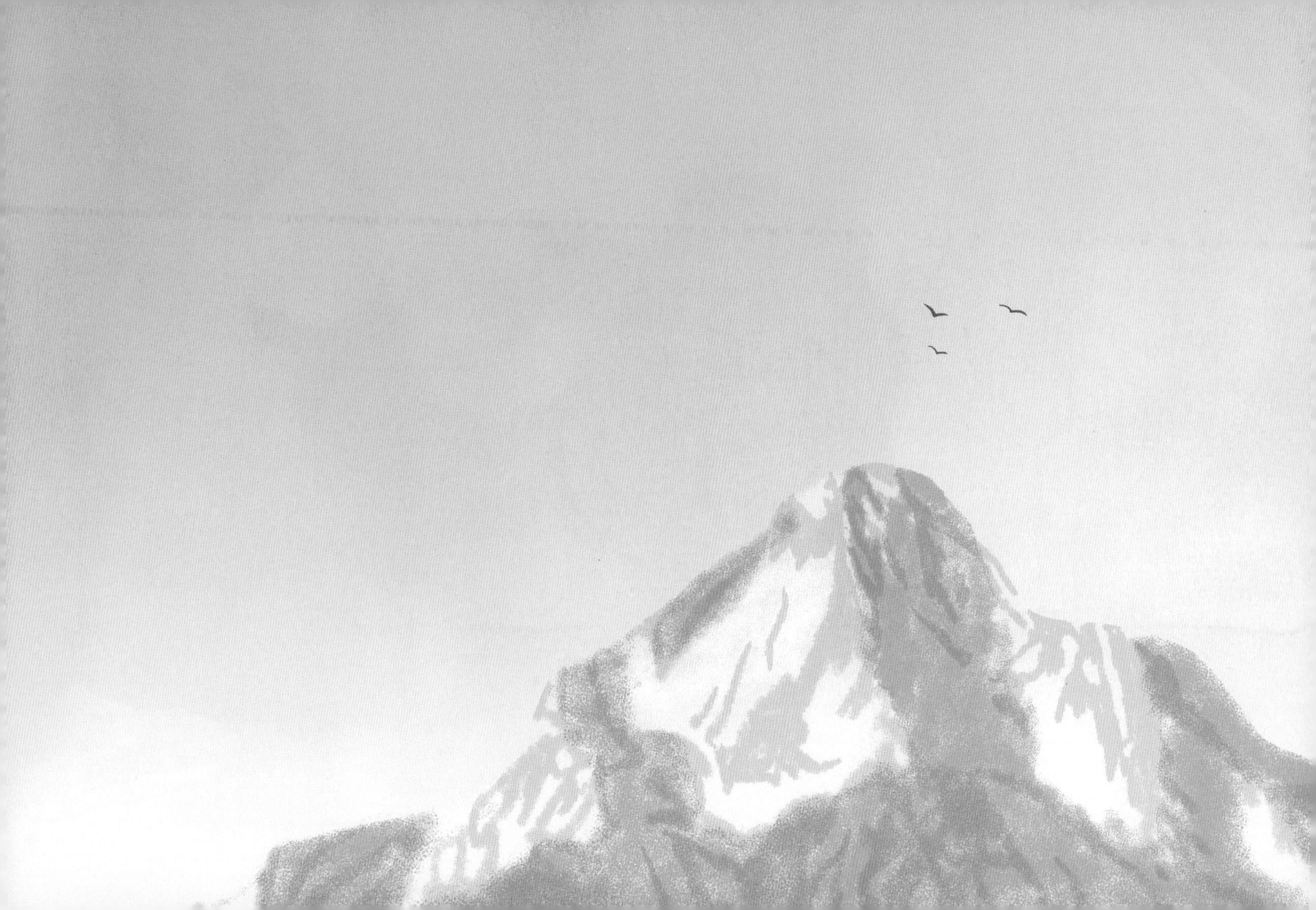

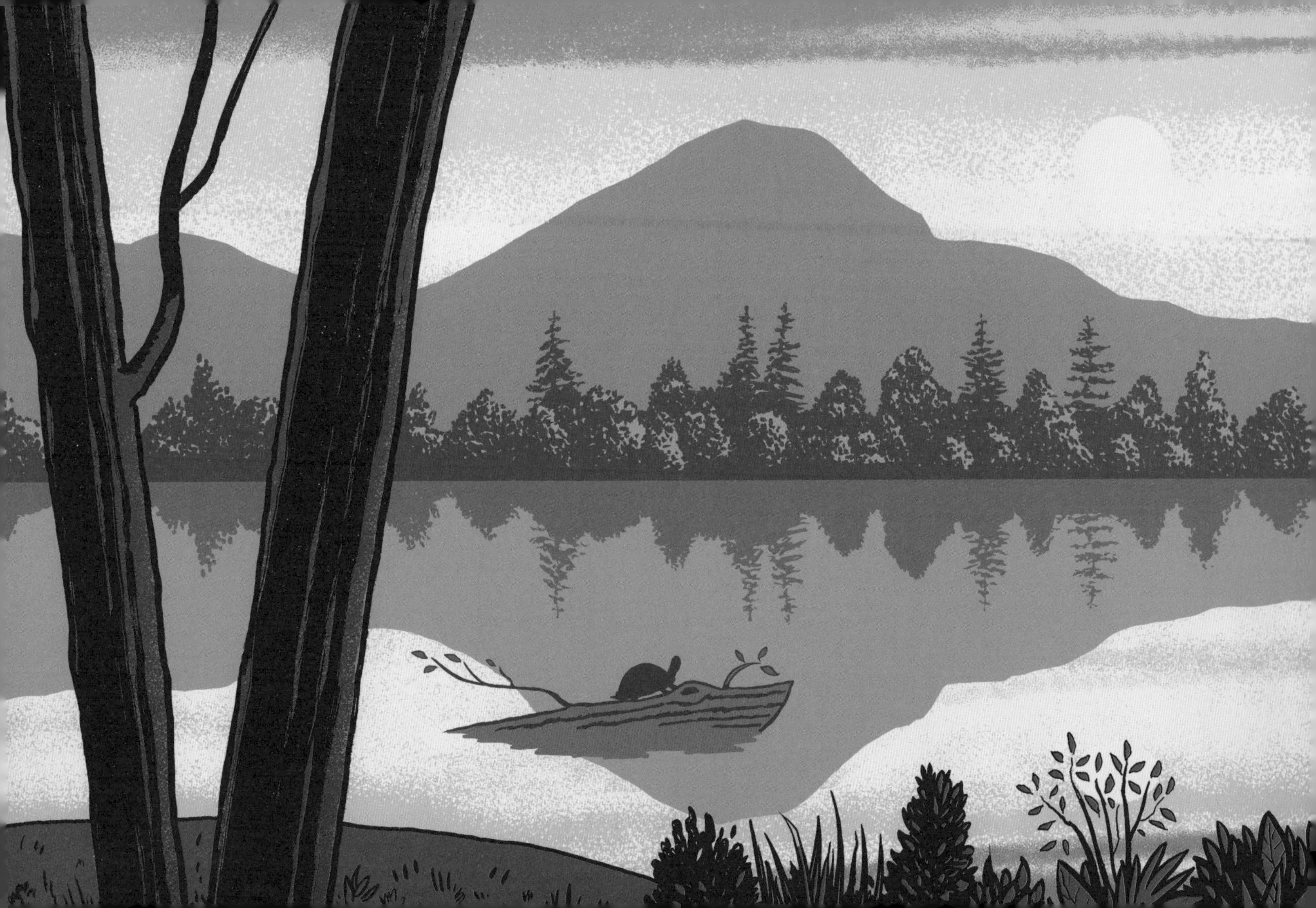

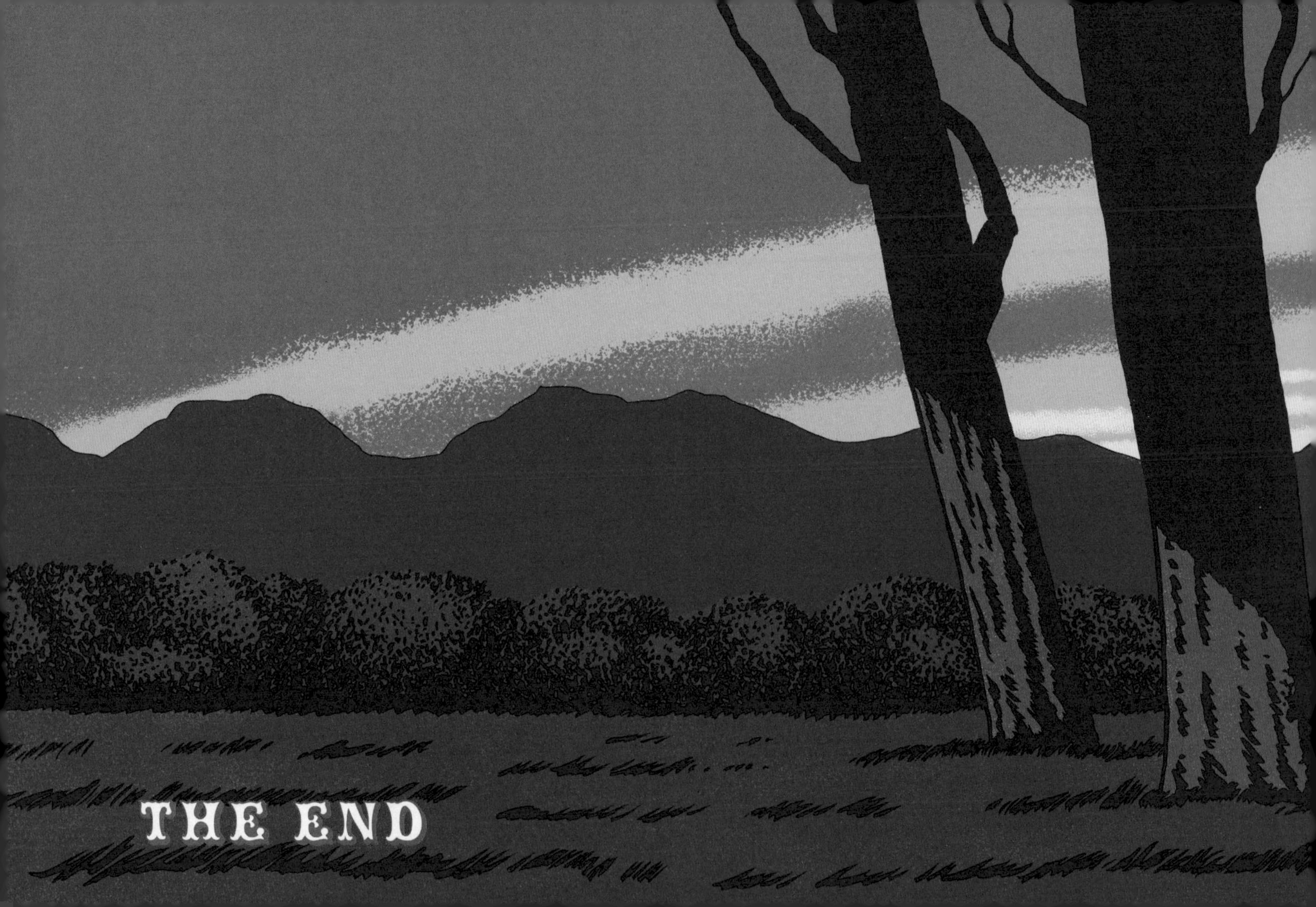
THE END

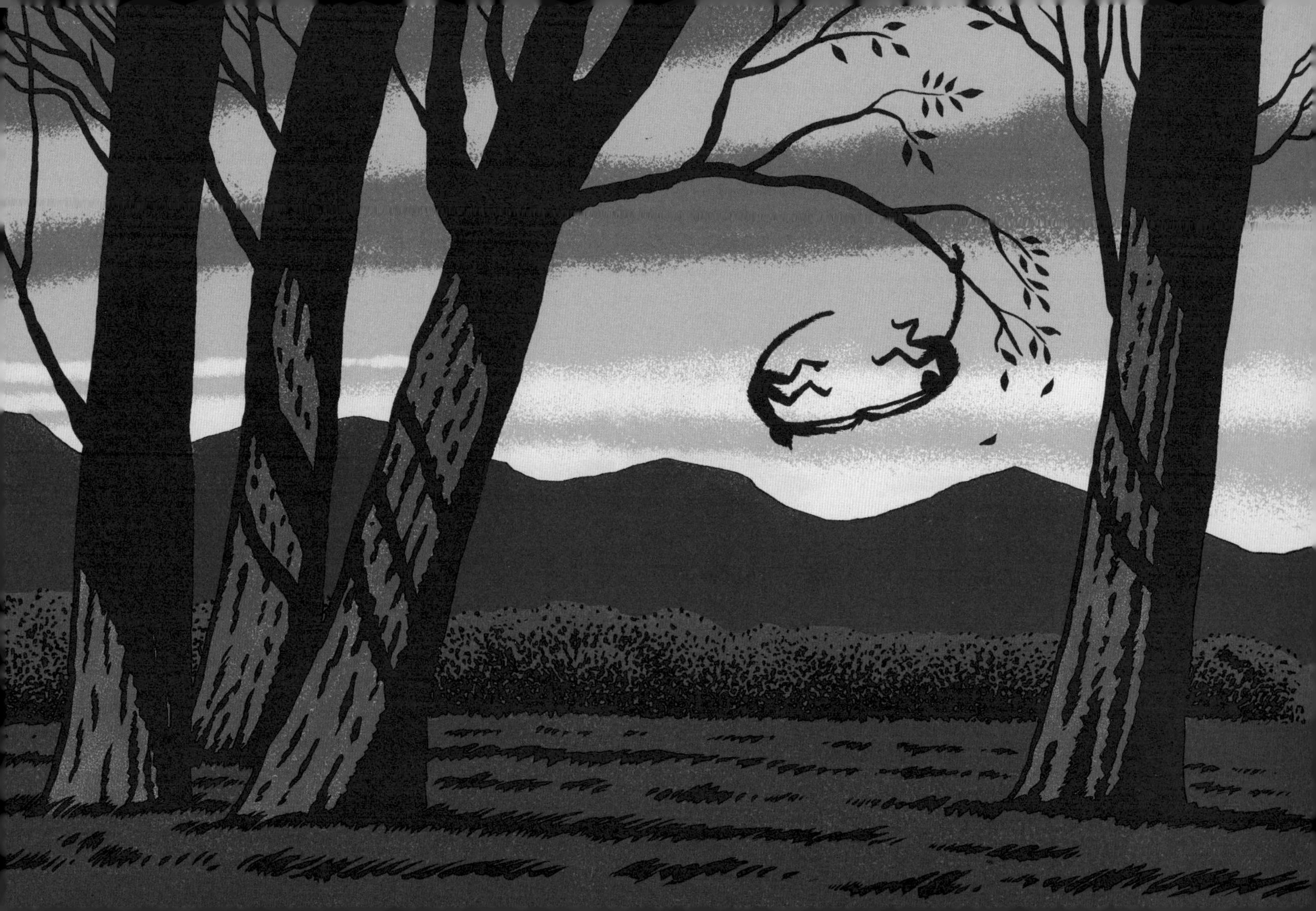

ABOUT KAMISHIBAI

More than a thousand years ago in Japan, Buddhist monks told stories using picture scrolls. Their stories often contained moral lessons. Since many in the audience couldn't read, the monks used pictures. As they told the story, the scrolls were slowly unspooled, and the audience "read" the pictures. This kind of storytelling was called *e-toki* (or "picture-explaining"). Starting in the late 1920s, a new form of *e-toki* emerged, inspired by silent films from the West.

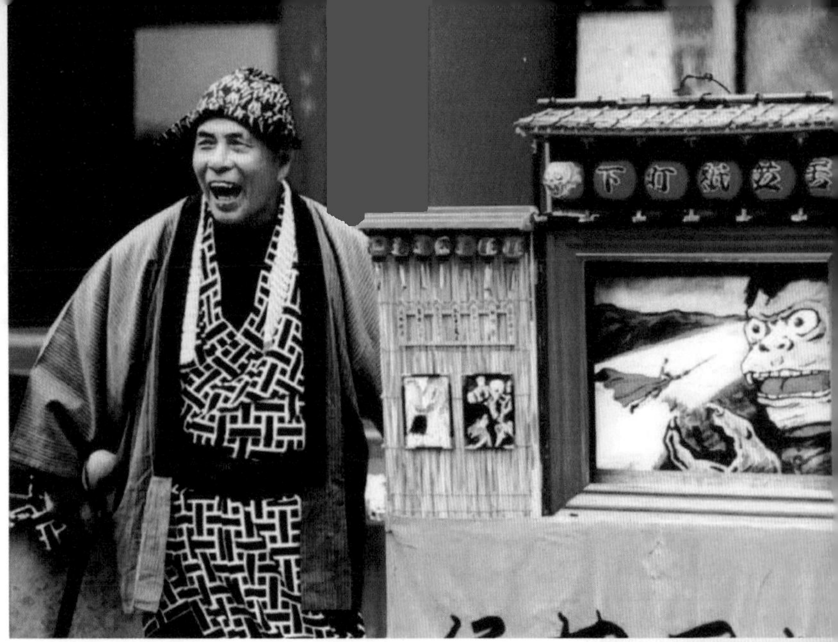

It was called *kamishibai* (or "paper theater"). Up until the mid-1950s, it wasn't unusual to see the *gaito kamishibaiya*, or *kamishibai* street performer, on his bicycle riding from village to village. The children would be alerted to the storyteller's arrival by the sound of two wooden clappers (called *hyoshigi*) banging together. The sound meant not only the telling of a story, but something equally as exciting—candy!

On the back of the storyteller's bike was a concession stand. The *gaito kamishibaiya* did not charge for

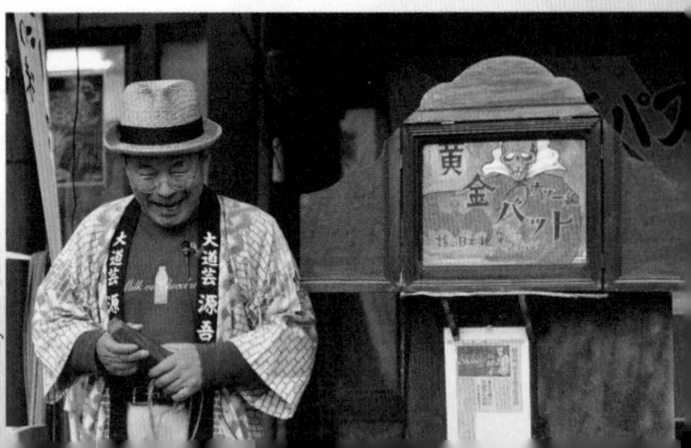
黄金
バット

Photo by Aki Sato

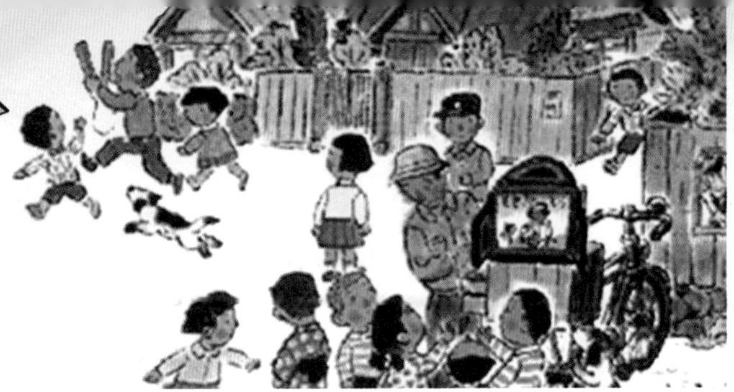

from www.kamishibai.com

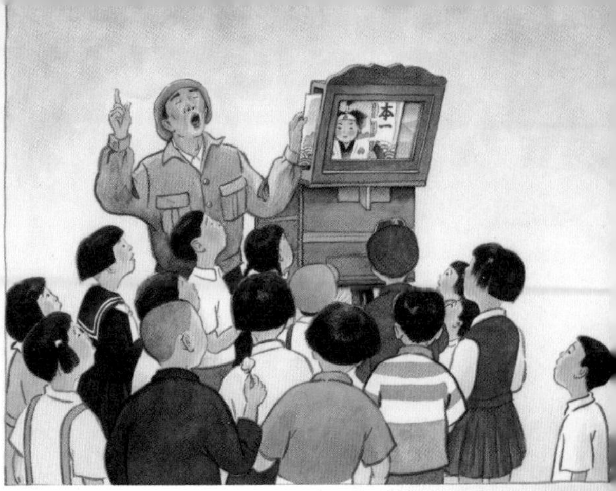
本一

from Kamishibai Man *by Allen Say*

their performances but sold candy to earn money, and the kids who bought some got to stand up front. The performer then opened a wooden box, strapped to the back of the bike. It unfolded to create a stage for a stack of illustrated boards. The drawings came to life as the storyteller revealed the cards one by one–accompanying each image with dialogue, sound effects, and sometimes even music.

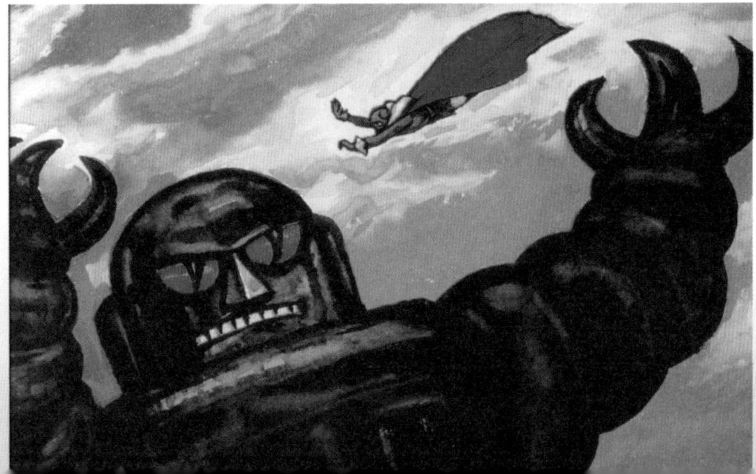

from Manga Kamishibai

So even before Batman and Superman were created in the U.S., Japanese children thrilled to the continuing adventures of the superheroes Ōgon (Golden) Bat and Prince of Gamma.

Storytellers would tell episodes from several different stories, always making sure to leave their audiences hanging at the most exciting part before folding up their stage and riding off to another village. That way, they could be sure that the children would want to come next time to hear more of the story.

ABOUT THE AUTHOR

JAMES STURM is the author of several books for kids, including the "Adventures in Cartooning" series (with Andrew Arnold and Alexis Frederick-Frost) and the forthcoming *Ape and Armadillo Take Over the World*. James also helped start a college for cartoonists, The Center for Cartoon Studies, in the small railroad village of White River Junction, Vermont. Here's what he has to say about *Birdsong*: "My friend Ben Matchstick shared with me his love for *kamishibai*. Ben even built his own folding wooden stage so he could perform *kamishibai*. I drew a story for Ben to perform that eventually became the pictures in this book. *Birdsong* has no words because it is meant to be performed. I wish Ben and I could ride our bikes into communities like the *gaito kamishibaiya* of old and visit every school and library and perform *Birdsong*. Unfortunately we both live in Vermont, which is a long bicycle ride to most places (plus I only like riding my bike downhill).

Since neither Ben nor I can perform this story in person, I am hoping **YOU** can be your own *gaito kamishibaiya*. So please read this book with others and take turns narrating. What do the monkeys say to one another? Do they make human or animal sounds? Or both? How loud does the tiger roar? What does the circus man say when releasing the monkeys? There is no correct way to perform this story, only your way. When you perform this story for a class, a parent, or a friend you are part of a tradition that goes back a long, long way. And like the stories the Buddhist monks told centuries ago, there might even be a moral lesson in these pictures as well."

from Manga Kamishibai

Ben Matchstick's folding stage

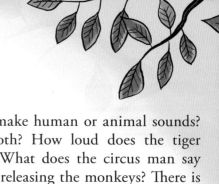

The drawings in this book were inspired by the sublime woodblock prints of William S. Rice.

Special thanks to Ben T. Matchstick for introducing me to the wonders of *kamishibai*. His *kamishibai* performance of *Birdsong* helped this book take flight.

I am also indebted to Tara McGowan for her generous encouragement and editorial feedback. In addition to being an accomplished *kamishibai* performer, Tara is America's peerless *kamishibai* scholar and advocate.

from Manga Kamishibai

FURTHER RESOURCES

KAMISHIBAI MAN; Allen Say. Houghton Mifflin, 2005. *The award-winning author remembers listening to* kamishibai *during his childhood in Japan.*

MANGA KAMISHIBAI: THE ART OF JAPANESE PAPER THEATER; Eric P. Nash. Abrams Comicarts, 2009. *An overview of the history of* kamishibai *with lots of great images.*

THE KAMISHIBAI CLASSROOM: ENGAGING MULTIPLE LITERACIES THROUGH THE ART OF PAPER THEATER; Tara McGowan. Libraries Unlimited, 2010. *An essential how-to for using* kamishibai *performance and story creation as a teaching tool.*

Online Resources:

ABOUTJAPAN.JAPANSOCIETY.ORG/
CONTENT.CFM/THE-MANY-FACES-OF-
KAMISHIBAI *An historical overview of* kamishibai *by Tara McGowan. The site includes many other resources, including Common Core-aligned lesson plans.*

WWW.KAMISHIBAI.COM *Many resources for teachers, including downloadable lesson plans.*

WWW.VTSHOME.ORG *Like* kamishibai, *this Visual Thinking Strategies website is great for educators who want to explore visual literacy.*

from Manga Kamishibai

from: www.kamishibai.com

TIPS FOR PARENTS AND TEACHERS:

HOW TO READ COMICS WITH KIDS

Kids love comics! They are naturally drawn to the details in the pictures, which make them want to read the words. Comics beg for repeated readings and let both emerging and reluctant readers enjoy complex stories with a rich vocabulary. But since comics have their own grammar, here are a few tips for reading them with kids:

GUIDE YOUNG READERS: Use your finger to show your place in the text, but keep it at the bottom of the speaking character so it doesn't hide the very important facial expressions.

HAM IT UP! Think of the comic book story as a play and don't hesitate to read with expression and intonation. Assign parts or get kids to supply the sound effects, a great way to reinforce phonics skills.

LET THEM GUESS. Comics provide lots of context for the words, so emerging readers can make informed guesses. Like jigsaw puzzles, comics ask readers to make connections, so check a young audience's understanding by asking "What's this character thinking?" (but don't be surprised if a kid finds some of the comics' subtle details faster than you).

TALK ABOUT THE PICTURES. Point out how the artist paces the story with pauses (silent panels) or speeded-up action (a burst of short panels). Discuss how the size and shape of the panels carry meaning.

ABOVE ALL, ENJOY! There is of course never one right way to read, so go for the shared pleasure. Once children make the story happen in their imagination, they have discovered the thrill of reading, and you won't be able to stop them. At that point, just go get them more books, and more comics.

www.TOON-BOOKS.com

SEE OUR FREE ONLINE CARTOON MAKERS, LESSON PLANS, AND MUCH MORE